MARCUS WAS R[illegible] HIS MIND, TRYING TO CR[illegible] EVERYTHING ELSE.

"Wow!" David said, looking down a steep precipice at the right of the road. "I guess you're a goner if you go off there."

"This is true," Marcus said. "So don't get drunk before the race, okay?"

"If you insist."

Marcus stopped the van and pointed to a flag at the top of the hill. "Now, there'll be four of these flags scattered around the course. Each one will be on a hilltop. Whoever crosses it first gains thirty seconds on his time. Understand? It's a way to get back some of the time you lost yesterday."

"What's the big deal, Marcus?" David turned and faced him. "You're winning. You don't need me."

Marcus put his hand on David's shoulder. "The big deal is that you're my brother."

David eyed him for a moment, then turned away.

"Got it?" Marcus asked.

"Got it."

A WW PRODUCTION
A JOHN BADHAM FILM

AMERICAN FLYERS

starring
KEVIN COSTNER
DAVID GRANT
RAE DAWN CHONG
ALEXANDRA PAUL
JANICE RULE

Director of Photography
DON PETERMAN, A.S.C.

Film Edited by
FRANK MORRISS

Music Score by
LEE RITENOUR & GREG MATHIESON

Written by
STEVE TESICH

Produced by
GARETH WIGAN & PAULA WEINSTEIN

Directed by
JOHN BADHAM

FROM **WARNER BROS** A WARNER COMMUNICATIONS COMPANY

AMERICAN FLYERS

Novel by Steven Phillip Smith

Based on the Film Written by
Steve Tesich

BANTAM BOOKS
TORONTO • NEW YORK • LONDON • SYDNEY • AUCKLAND

AMERICAN FLYERS

A Bantam Book / August 1985

ISBN 0-553-25262-3

Published simultaneously in the United States and Canada

Bantam Books are published by Bantam Books, Inc. Its trademark, consisting of the words "Bantam Books" and the portrayal of a rooster, is Registered in U.S. Patent and Trademark Office and in other countries. Marca Registrada. Bantam Books, Inc., 666 Fifth Avenue, New York, New York 10103.

PRINTED IN THE UNITED STATES OF AMERICA

O 0 9 8 7 6 5 4 3 2 1

AMERICAN FLYERS

1

Although he had no special training route, the more days David Sommers rode, the more familiar he became with the network of two-lane blacktop highways that radiated outward from St. Louis like spokes on the wheel of his bicycle. Today he had crossed the river, sprinted through the ghetto of East St. Louis, Illinois (barely missing a slow freight lumbering along the tracks by a housing project), then pedaled another forty miles out into the flat Illinois farm country. There had been rain that morning, and although the sun was out while he rode, the humid air was thick as gravy. It didn't matter. There was only the initial discomfort (as there was with cold or rain or even snow) which usually vanished as he broke a sweat and his thighs began to burn. As his chest began to heave and his heart pounded like a little drum, he had brief fantasies of coronary failure or blood vessels bursting in his head, but once he settled into a rhythm his thoughts of disaster gave way to competitive ferocity. He left imaginary foreigners gasping for air behind him as he crossed finish line after finish line ahead of the pack, waving to crowds that cheered him on. Between races he transformed himself into Jesse James on horseback, leading his band out to the hinterlands to liberate gold from greedy financiers. David thought that the James/Younger Gang had robbed banks in Centralia and Vandalia. Perhaps they'd ridden the same road he was on, before the pavement came.

"Look at them faggoty pants."

David had just finished an excruciating race through the mountains of France, and he looked up to see two winos enjoying a short-dog of Thunderbird as they sat in what was left of a battered couch that had been abandoned by the side of the road. One of them was pointing at David and laughing, looking as at home as though he were in his living room watching TV.

"Go get 'em, cowboy," the other man said.

David tipped the brim of his Western hat and managed a smile as the men slapped hands and exploded with drunken guffaws. "I'll do my best," he muttered. But tired from his defeat of the great racers of Europe, he did not exert himself until he was out of Illinois and high on the bridge crossing the Mississippi.

The river. David Sommers loved the sight of it, the brown water gliding relentlessly by St. Louis, midway on its journey from Minnesota to New Orleans. Even though he could see the Mississippi from his mother's condominium (his family had moved into the high-rise after their home had been nearly obliterated by the flood of 1973), he still made it a point to go near the water every day. It brought him up, filled him with a wonderful sense of adventure and of life's potential. On the days that he rode only along the river, he would forget his outlaw heroes and give himself over to the explorer side of his personality, becoming DeSoto, LaSalle, Marquette and Joliet, and experiencing some of the amazement they must have felt as they explored this magnificent waterway.

As he came off the bridge and started up the street, he began to hum "Git Along, Little Dogies" and pedal a little faster. He finished a verse, and the glistening white Delta Queen-type steamboat a quarter-mile upriver let out a long, low blast on its whistle which David experienced as prolonged, mocking flatulence. The paddle wheel splashed up water in a manner that suggested laughter, and David felt suddenly challenged. Just as suddenly he began to move. With one eye on the road and the other on the boat, he stood up and sprinted, allowing a brief moment to see himself as a riverboat gambler—maybe Rex Harrison in *The Foxes of Harrow*—dealing faro and dispatching cheaters with the derringer hidden in his boot. He caught the boat within a minute, pulling up even, raising his fist in yet another triumphant gesture, then turning off and starting toward home.

He was in no hurry. There wouldn't be much to do when he got there. School was out for the summer, and he didn't feel much like seeing anyone he knew. But he'd been feeling like that for a while. Slowly drifting away. Even the enthusiasts in his Oriental philosophy class left him kind of cold. Talk, talk, talk—that's all they ever did. If Oriental philosophy had taught him anything, it was that you didn't need to talk. Maybe he'd go down to the Criterion after dinner and catch the double bill of *The Magnificent Seven* and *One-Eyed Jacks,* even though he'd seen each of them more than ten times. You can't get too much of a good thing.

He stopped beneath the famous Gateway Arch, straddling his bicycle and gazing straight up to the apex of the gleaming steel monument. St. Louis. The gateway to the West. The Arch always caused him to experience a variety of feelings. Sometimes it seemed ugly and stupid, a colossal waste of space and money—he could imagine it painted gold, the cornerstone of the world's largest McDonald's. Other times, the Arch took on a cold and stunning beauty, and David felt a great reverence for the courage and endurance of the men and women who ventured into the uncharted wilds of the American West. He tipped his hat in salute to Lewis and Clark, Jim Bridger and the mountain men, shaking his head in wonder at what they must have had to endure. He probably wouldn't have lasted a week. Maybe he'd take a little trip this summer if it looked like his mother wouldn't get too lonely without him.

He cruised slowly through the park, watching busy people hurrying through and un-busy people lounging on the benches or dozing on the grass. David felt that he was somehow in the middle—busy doing nothing. Perhaps he had achieved the perfect fusion of the yin and the yang. Then again, perhaps he wasn't doing doodle-e-squat.

Back on the street, he stopped for a red light and looked down the block. A man came out of his building in a neatly pressed three-piece suit. He walked jauntily to the curb where a passing (and ancient) Chevy Impala splashed much of a puddle of water onto his immaculate front. The man kept cool, giving David an Oliver Hardy look that said it all. David dropped his head so the man wouldn't see him smiling.

He heard a roaring engine, and looked up to see a mammoth garbage truck round the corner and bear down on the puddle. The sense of challenge seemed to rise in David instantaneously, and as the man backed away from the curb, David shot forward on his bicycle, racing to beat the truck to the puddle as though his life depended on it. His hat blew off his head, but the string kept it attached to him. He seemed to close on the puddle in an instant, shooting past and stopping as the garbage truck sent a small tidal wave onto the sidewalk. David felt two drops hit the back of his leg.

"Bravo!" The man tucked his briefcase beneath his arm and applauded. David shrugged, circling back and stopping on the sidewalk facing the building. The man started forward, then stopped. David knew that he himself should be moving, but before the message could get to his legs he was drenched. He turned to watch the blue Volvo depart quietly down the street, then faced the smiling man. He stepped forward and patted David on the shoulder. "It happens in the best of families." They both burst out laughing, and David kept on laughing most of the way home.

He sprinted the last six blocks, slowing as he turned onto his street so Mr. Treadway would have plenty of time to see him coming. The aging doorman waved once, and by the time David got to the building the door was wide open. "Thank you, Mr. Treadway," David said, rolling through the entry. He skirted the Oriental carpet in the middle of the marble-walled foyer, scooped the pile of mail off the table beneath the gilt-edged mirror, then rode into the elevator behind an old man and woman. In one fluid movement he dismounted and stood his bicycle up beside him as though it were another person. The couple looked a little frightened. The man smiled nervously and said, "Good afternoon, David."

"Hi, Mr. Shank." David nodded at the woman. "Mrs. Shank."

"Hello, David." She seemed appalled by him. Maybe it was his sogginess.

"I was out riding," he said.

Mr. and Mrs. Shank nodded politely.

"Got splashed." He opened the large manila envelope addressed to him and pulled out the contents. On top of a stack of eight-by-ten glossies was a note: "Dear David, Would you be a dear and show these to your mother. Love, Vera."

David shook his head and slid the note off the pictures. It was Vera, all right. Wearing very little and looking very good. David let out a low moan at the thought of her lovely body, and he shook his head over what a calculating little bitch she was. He looked up to see both Mr. and Mrs. Shank staring over his shoulder, his face full of interest, hers of disapproval—the yin and the yang of lust.

David forced a smile. "She told me she was majoring in political science." The bell rang and the elevator stopped. "See you later." David lowered his bike, climbed on, and rode down the hallway.

He stopped in front of his mother's place, staying on his bike as he unlocked the door. He pushed it open and pedaled into the living room, seemingly unable to get off his bike and walk. He liked his "condo ride," his final warm-down, and a chance to do some fancy maneuvering around his mother's ever-changing high-tech furniture. She was in the fashion business and had to keep abreast of all the latest fads. Long ago David had stopped telling her that she didn't have to live with the fads as well.

The phone rang, but as he was not expecting any calls—or wanting any, for that matter—David let it ring until the answering machine took over. Modern conveniences! In a few years, people wouldn't even have to get out of bed by themselves.

"Hello. You have reached the Sommers' residence." David's mother's voice had just the right blend of warmth and professionalism. "Nobody is in at the moment, but if you leave a message, we'll get back to you as soon as possible."

David was threading his way between the dining room

table and the china cabinet when the beep sounded. "Hi, Mom. It's Marcus."

"Marcus!" David shouted, his stomach feeling suddenly hollow. He wheeled around the table, hitting the brakes in the living room. His skill failed him, and he toppled over, taking an end table with him. The lamp landed on his back as he began crawling for the phone. "Marcus!"

"I figured it was time we saw each other again," Marcus said.

"Shit!" David bellowed. His feet were strapped into the pedals, and he couldn't get them out. He felt as if he were trapped in quicksand as he struggled to get to the phone.

"I'm on the road right now," Marcus said. "I should be in St. Louis by dinnertime. 'Bye."

"Don't hang up!" David managed to get to the phone and lift the receiver in time to hear a click at the other end. "Marcus!" he yelled. Nothing. "Jesus," he muttered, hanging up the phone. He lay on the floor for a moment, feeling disappointed, then shrugged it off. No big deal. His older brother Marcus was on his way to St. Louis. He'd be here tonight. That was the important thing. He got untangled from his bike and stood up. Tonight! Great! He leaned the bike against the couch, then returned the end table and lamp to their proper positions. Lucky he didn't bang his head and brain himself. No sense in hurrying the inevitable. He gave a little whoop of joy at the thought of seeing Marcus, then headed for his room.

He tossed the pictures of Vera onto the bed—he wouldn't be seeing her there in the flesh again—picked up the phone and dialed his mother's office. Might as well prepare her, he thought. He guessed you could say that Marcus and his mother were "estranged."

"Sommers Modeling Agency."

"Louise, it's David." He could see Louise, a little too old and a little too heavy to be a model, sitting behind her immaculate desk, facing at least a dozen young beauties desperate for his mother's favor.

"Hi, Davey."

"How's the meat rack?"

"Loaded," Louise said. "Want some phone numbers?"
"Never again."
"Smart kid. Want to talk to your mom?"
"If she's free."
"I'll squeeze you in on line four."
Click. Silence. Another click. "Davey?" His mother's voice had an anxious edge—she could never quite conceal her fear.
"Alive and ticking."
"Don't make jokes."
"Sorry, Mom."
"What's going on? I'm very busy."
David turned away from his poster of the outlaw Josey Wales to one of Marcus winning a bicycle race. "Mom, guess who's coming home to dinner?"
After a moment, she said, "Marcus?" The anxiety was back.
"You sound thrilled."
"Well . . ."
"He's your first-born son, Mom. Aren't you happy?"
"Of course I'm happy, Davey."
"Me too."
"I'll bet you are."
"Try to get home early, huh?"
"I will. Gotta run."
"Mom?"
"What?"
"Think peace. Okay?"
She hesitated for a moment. "Okay," she said. "See you in a bit."
David hung up the phone, took a deep breath, and looked around his room. "Peace, please," he mumbled, rubbing the tops of his thighs. He stood up and did a couple of stretches, then lifted his bike and hung it on the wall hooks. "What it is, Bro," he said, staring at the picture of himself and Marcus on the wall. David was sitting in a bright red wagon that had "American Flyer" written on the side. He was dressed in a cowboy outfit, smiling and waving at the camera, indescribably happy that his older brother (also in

cowboy garb) had consented to pull him around with his bicycle. With nine years between them, David hadn't gotten to play with Marcus too much while he was growing up, and he still treasured those moments that his older brother spent with him. David had often been a pest, but Marcus had been as patient and protective as one could expect a teen-age brother to be.

His room looked like a pigpen, and he went around it quickly, piling the dirty laundry in the middle of the carpet, closing his bureau drawers and straightening things up. He stopped in front of his desk, shaking his head at the copy of the article on "Berry Aneurysm" that lay beside his book on Western movies. He quickly hid the article in the middle of another stack of books. He didn't want Marcus seeing it and thinking that he was getting morbid or something worse. Feeling a sudden pull toward depression, he popped a Springsteen tape into his cassette player, putting the rhythm in his walk as he crossed the room to his bed. He sat right on Vera's smiling face. "Sorry, baby," he muttered. He reached under the bed and pulled out his little American Flyer wagon which held his bike tools and extra pairs of shoes and gloves. He smiled at the wagon, then put today's equipment in and gently pushed it back. Then he half stood up, whipping off his shorts and firing them into the closet before coming down on Vera once again. Naked, he stood up and headed for the shower, a glossy shot of Vera hugging his behind.

2

Marcus didn't show up for dinner, and as David and his mother finished their salad the empty place at the table became more and more conspicuous, and Mrs. Sommers' mood (and look) of vulnerable anxiety was rapidly being replaced by an irritation that bordered on downright anger. She looked at her watch and shook her head. "I guess we might as well move on to the main course."

"Don't get upset, Mom." More than anything, David wanted to keep the lid on.

"It's typical." She huffed out to the kitchen with the salad plates, returning in a moment with their dinners of whitefish, rice, and Brussels sprouts.

"Looks good, Mom."

She made some unintelligible groan, then took an angry bite.

"Maybe he had car trouble."

Mrs. Sommers shrugged. "Maybe."

"I mean, it happens."

"He could've called."

"Maybe he's on a road with no phones." David was beginning to feel irritated with Marcus himself.

"Sure," she said. "And maybe he just changed his mind again. Decided not to pollute his soul with our, uh, *my* awful presence."

"Come on, Mom."

"It's damn inconsiderate."

"He didn't say he'd be here *precisely* at dinnertime. It sounded kind of tentative."

"You don't have to defend him."

"He's my brother." David took a bite of fish and smiled at his mother. "Good eats."

She nodded distractedly. Her mind was somewhere else.

Let her be, David thought. He knew that anything he said would only make things worse.

Marcus Sommers eased his van over to the curb about fifty feet before the entrance to his mother's building. He resisted an impulse to turn around and head back to Wisconsin, then killed the engine and set the emergency brake. He sat in the darkness for a moment, trying to dispel the cloud of negativity that had been getting thicker and thicker the closer he got to his mother's. He had decided to skip dinner with her, stopping instead at Koslow's Kafé, the favorite greasy spoon of his youth, where the motto was "Simple But Good," and where the chicken-fried steak, mashed potatoes and gravy, and hot apple pie had nearly made him happy to be back in St. Louis again. After eating, he had driven around town for an hour, cruising by his old haunts, hoping that a flood of nostalgia would finally overcome his bitter feelings.

No such luck, he thought, pounding the dashboard with the palm of his hand. "You might as well face it, buddy," he mumbled, then reached into the rear of the van and grabbed his duffel bag. He picked up the bouquet of flowers he had bought before dinner and climbed out into the humid night. On the sidewalk, he looked at the flowers and shook his head, experiencing an uncomfortable combination of nervousness, depression, and anger. No good, he thought, tossing the flowers into a garbage can. Too much like a peace offering or an admission of guilt. He decided simply to play it straight. No frills.

"Hey there, Mr. Treadway," he said as he approached the doorway.

"Marcus!" the doorman said, rising from his stool and shaking Marcus's hand. "Good to see you. David told me you'd be coming."

"I'm a little late."

"They'll be glad to see you. Any special reason for the visit?"

"Probably not that important." Marcus smiled. "How's the world been treating you, Mr. Treadway?"

The doorman shrugged. "Can't complain. A little stiff with the arthritis in the mornings."

"You ought to try taking alfalfa."

Mr. Treadway looked at him suspiciously. "I thought that was for horses."

Marcus smiled and patted him on the shoulder. "You ever hear of a horse complaining of arthritis?"

The doorman laughed, shaking his head. "You're something else, Marcus. You still racing that bicycle?"

"Sure. Got a big one coming up."

"Your brother's going to town on his."

"Really?"

Mr. Treadway nodded. "Gone most of every day. At least he says he's riding."

"Good for him."

"Had a couple of pretty nice-looking girls over too."

"Even better."

"That's right. I told him I'd take any extras off his hands."

Marcus laughed. "That'd probably help you out more than alfalfa."

"I'd say so. Might give me a heart attack though."

"Not a bad way to go."

"Amen."

"Well," Marcus said. "Guess I better get up there and say hello."

"Good to see you, Marcus. Probably see you tomorrow."

"No doubt."

Mr. Treadway held the door open, and Marcus took a deep breath and started for the elevator.

Ah, the pregnant silence, David thought. With his fork he pushed his last sprout around his plate as though it were a hockey puck. He wondered what his mother was thinking. Rehearsing the past once again? Blaming Marcus? Justifying herself? David wanted all the blame to vanish, wanted peace with honor on all sides.

"Do you have to keep doing that?" his mother snapped.

"No." David smiled, then popped the vegetable in his mouth, trying to smile while he chewed, trying to show with his eyes that he meant everything to be all right. His good will seemed to have little effect; her icy expression didn't alter one bit.

David swallowed, gave a contented groan and rubbed his stomach. "You know what, Mom?"

She eyed him suspiciously. "No."

"I think I'm breaking through one of those psychological barriers."

"I don't understand." She didn't look like she wanted to, either.

"You know," he said, "the way people do when they suddenly start enjoying German opera and Japanese movies."

She shook her head. "What do you mean?"

He wiped his mouth and smiled. "I'm finally starting to like Brussels sprouts."

After a moment she smiled. He winked at her in triumph. Then the doorbell rang, and they both gave little jumps as if someone had frightened them. In a way, someone had.

David fought his urge to leap up, casually dropping his napkin on the table and rising slowly. "I'll get it," he said casually.

She nodded, all the stiffness back in her face.

He walked slowly until he was out of her line of sight, then he bolted for the door. He stopped in front of it, taking a couple of deep breaths and checking himself in the mirror. He stuck out his tongue. What the hell was he doing? This was his brother, not a goddamn date. He opened the door and peered out. Marcus looked great—lean, fit, intelligent, and his mustache made him appear very mature. David envied his togetherness, the way he always seemed to be able to take care of everything. "Yes?" David said. "May I help you?" He opened the door all the way.

He tried to keep a stone face, but as Marcus's smile broadened, David felt his own doing the same.

"You bastard." Marcus stepped forward and the brothers embraced.

"You son of a bitch." David squeezed him tightly. He felt incredibly glad to have him back home. "It's about time you showed your face around here."

Marcus pushed away and took a good look at David. "It's good to see you. You lost weight."

"No, I didn't." David shook his head. "You lost touch. I got taller."

"Whatever," Marcus said. "You look great." He put his arm around David and they started out of the entry hall. Suddenly Marcus stopped, taking a look around. He let out a little groan of disgust, then whispered, "Who poured ugly all over the walls?" The stripes were not to his liking.

David felt a momentary panic, as though something bad were beginning. ''Mom just wallpapered half the place.''

Marcus held his nose.

''Tell her you like it,'' David pleaded. ''Please.''

Instantly he could tell that Marcus didn't like getting marching orders from him. David shot him a brief apologetic glance, Marcus nodded, and the two brothers started for the dining room. ''He's here, Mom!'' David bellowed proudly.

He led Marcus into the dining room where their mother was standing beside her chair. David couldn't quite decide if she looked more like a mannequin or a junior high school girl waiting for her first date.

''Hi, Mom.'' Marcus broke the ice.

''Hello, Marcus.'' Another crack.

''Sorry I'm late.'' He stopped a couple of feet before her chair.

''It's all right.''

''I got held up.''

She shrugged and gave him a little smile. ''Welcome home.''

David watched as his mother and brother smiled sheepishly at each other, then each came forward the necessary foot so they could kiss. No arms around each other and not a whole lot of warmth, but it was a kiss—a start. Marcus's eyes met David's, and David smiled.

Marcus turned back to his mother. ''New wallpaper,'' he said, looking around.

''We just got it.''

''It's really nice.''

David coughed, trying to suppress a laugh.

''I'm glad you like it,'' Mrs. Sommers said. She seemed to believe him. ''Sit down, Marcus.'' She gestured to a chair and began to sit down herself. ''I think the fish is still warm.''

Marcus sat, but when she reached for his plate, he politely put up his hand. ''I already ate on the road, Mom. Got hungry.''

Mrs. Sommers nodded with disappointment. ''In that case, I might as well clear these.'' She began to get up.

"Wait!" David grabbed his own dishes. "I'll take care of this." He cleared her place as though he were a professional waiter. "Why don't you two, uh, you know. Talk."

"Don't you want some coffee?" his mother asked.

"I'll get some later."

"You don't have to . . ."

"I'm doing it," David interrupted. He strode into the kitchen and put the dishes on the counter by the sink. He returned with another load, and although he was able to save the serving dish when it dropped, what remained of the Brussels sprouts splattered onto the immaculate kitchen floor. "Great," he muttered, bending down to pick up the errant sprouts. He rose and started for the trash bucket, then the dizziness came on him so suddenly that he almost fell on the floor. He grabbed the counter, lowering his head and breathing heavily. He didn't need this now—he didn't want Marcus seeing him this way, that was for sure. The spells had been happening every two or three weeks over the past year, and he never knew when they were going to come. He couldn't figure it. He could go ride his bicycle for three or four hours and nothing ever happened, then he'd bend down to pick up some crummy vegetable and nearly turn into one himself. His heart was pounding—probably out of fear—but after a couple of minutes it began to slow, and his equilibrium returned. Just like that. No fuss, no muss. The walking time bomb.

He went to the utility closet and got the bucket and mop, also putting on the painter's cap that he found there. After filling the bucket, he put it down by the residue from the sprouts on the floor. As he began to hum "The Streets of Laredo," he pulled out the mop too fast, tipping over the bucket. "Goddammit!" he bellowed as the water cascaded across the floor.

"Everything all right in there?" his mother yelled.

He took a breath. "Under control." *I nearly died and now I can't even mop the floor properly.*

"We're going in the study for coffee if you need us."

"I'll be fine," he said. He was glad they had a cleaning woman. He didn't think he could do this mopping on a regular basis.

* * *

Always the elegant lady, Mrs. Sommers served the coffee in a silver pot with her best china. Marcus watched her as she poured. She was still a beautiful woman, aging well. It was a shame she had to look so cold and unhappy. He wondered if she was that way all the time, or if her doleful countenance had more to do with seeing him again.

"Do you still take it black?" She offered him a cup.

"Great. Thanks." He took it from her and looked around the room. It had been his father's study, and it had a much more masculine feel than the rest of the house. Warm and dark.

"Welcome back," she said. It was as if she couldn't think of anything else to say.

He nodded and toasted her with his coffee. "Nice to be back here again." He glanced around the room. "I'm really glad you didn't change Dad's study. I've always liked this room."

She almost shuddered. "It's always felt a little too dark in here for me."

Why did she have to say that? It almost felt like a challenge to him. He shrugged. "I guess I find it peaceful."

"I find it depressing."

He fought an urge to say something nasty, taking a sip of coffee instead. The fact was that she *hadn't* changed the room, no matter how depressing she found it. There must have been some reason for that.

"How long can you stay?" she asked.

"Not long." He took another drink, then leaned back and gave her a long look. Might as well spit it out, he thought. No other way to go about things. "You see, I came home to tell you, uh, well . . ." He trailed off, staring at the floor and shaking his head. "This is harder than I thought."

She smiled at him.

"You see, Mom, I . . ."

She held up her hand to stop him. "There's no need to apologize, Marcus. Can't we just . . ."

"Apologize!?" he exploded, suddenly full of rage. "I have nothing to apologize for!" He pointed at her. "If anybody should ap . . ." He stopped, shaking his head. He wasn't going to get into this. He probably shouldn't have come. "Let's skip it, Mom." He swallowed hard. "I came home because I'm worried about Davey."

She looked at him for a moment, saying nothing, almost as if she was weighing something in her mind. "What about Davey?"

"I think he should get out of here."

"You do, huh?" She glared at him.

"You bet."

"Why?" She had that edge of contempt in her voice.

"Oh, come on, Mom."

"Answer my question."

"He should go away to college, that's why. It's nothing against you, but college isn't a time you should spend living with your mother."

"And where would you suggest he go?"

"Anywhere. I don't care. As long as it's a good place. And my offer still stands. I'll pay for his last two years—if he transfers."

"Such generosity." She looked away.

"It's not . . ."

"Marcus," she interrupted, "for your information, David is doing just fine where he is."

Marcus stared at her for a moment. "He is *not* doing fine."

"He is, too."

"He's flunking out!"

She jerked her head as though someone had slapped her. "How do you know?"

"I have friends on the faculty. So don't try to tell me he's doing fine."

She gave him a hurt look. "He *could* be if . . ."

"Shit!" Marcus said.

She glanced at him balefully, then stood up and started to leave. He leaped to his feet and grabbed her by the arm. "Don't!" she said.

"Could be!" he said, his face inches from hers. "Oh, Christ! *Could* is still the operative word around here. *I* could've. *You* could've. *Dad* could've. And now it's Davey's turn." He exhaled with disgust. "We're always looking for alibis." His mother squirmed in his grip, trying to get loose. He felt like breaking her arm. "I'll tell you what we *could've*!" he growled. "You and I could be crazy about each other." He paused for a moment to let it sink in. "And you could've made Dad's last few weeks a lot easier."

She blinked rapidly a few times. "Must you keep reminding me? Don't you think I know?" She made a move as though she were trying to hit him. He dropped her arm, hoping she would, but she just stood there, all the fight seemingly gone.

He shook his head. "You probably won't believe this, but I came home hoping we wouldn't fight for once." He almost laughed out loud. How long had they managed without a fight, ten minutes?

"I don't give a damn why you came home," she said. "I've learned to live without you." Her voice cracked. "It's Davey that . . ." Her voice broke completely, and she sat down and sobbed.

Marcus watched her, wishing this hadn't happened, cursing himself for being so childish that it had. "Davey's a smart kid, Mom. He just needs to get out of here."

Gradually her crying stopped, and she looked up at Marcus as though he were a naive child. "And you call yourself a doctor."

"What's that supposed to mean?"

"Couldn't you tell just by looking at him?"

"Doctors aren't psychics, Mom. Tell what?"

She appealed to the ceiling. "Tell what, he asks."

"What the hell's the matter with him?" Marcus demanded.

"He thinks he's dying, that's what."

Marcus eyed her for a moment, trying to take this in. Twenty-year-old kids don't think they're dying. He opened his mouth to speak, but was stopped by the ringing of the phone.

"I'll get it," Mrs. Sommers said.

Marcus reached out and grabbed her arm. "Let Davey get it. He'll call if it's for you." He sat down and took a deep breath. "Now tell me what this is all about."

She smoothed the front of her dress, then gave him a sad look. "Davey thinks he has Berry aneurysm like your father did."

"And what put that idea into his head?" Marcus was trying to be patient, but he didn't know if he could handle it.

"The symptoms. He's not a hypochondriac."

"What symptoms, Mom?"

"You know, weight loss, dizziness, headaches. He thinks he's going to die."

Marcus exhaled long and steadily, then rubbed his hand over his face as though he were trying to rid himself of all troublesome visions. You're a professional, Marcus, he told himself. Now act like one. He leaned forward in his chair, trying his best to keep up a good bedside manner. "Kids lose weight for all kinds of reasons, Mom."

"Don't try to smooth anything over."

He shook his head. "I'm not. I just want to give you the facts."

"I think I'm acquainted with those."

He pretended not to hear her. "The dizziness could come from an ear infection or even a bad diet. And it's real common for kids to develop psychosomatic symptoms after the death of somebody they loved."

"Are you trying to tell me that he's imagining all this?"

"Not at all. It's probably very real to him. But it does happen. Especially if the person knows that the disease is inheritable."

"I don't know," Mrs. Sommers said wearily.

"I do, Mom. I went through some of the same symptoms myself."

"You?" She almost laughed. "The impervious Marcus?"

"Maybe not so impervious as you think." He cleared his throat. "How's Davey been acting?"

"He just wants to be alone," she sighed. "Nothing seems to matter to him. All he's done since school let out is ride that bike you gave him."

"That's not going to hurt him."

"Maybe not. But it isolates him. And he's got all these medical journals in his room. It's as if he's saying good-bye to the world.'' She dabbed away a couple of tears with a piece of tissue. ''It's all there in his eyes.''

''Ah, yes,'' Marcus muttered. ''The eyes.''

''What?''

''Mom, you don't diagnose Berry aneurysm by the look in somebody's eye.''

''Oh, I know,'' she said impatiently.

''Well?''

''Well what?''

''Uh, have you thought of taking him to the hospital and having him checked out?'' The steps in logic people missed amazed him.

''He's terrified of hospitals.''

''So are most people.''

''I just couldn't . . .'' Her voice trailed off and she threw up her hands.

''I'm a doctor, Mom. Why the hell didn't you call me?'' This situation was getting more absurd by the minute.

''Because you're the last person I could turn to.'' She sounded almost casual.

''That's great,'' he said.

''And I kept hoping that the symptoms would go away.''

''Um-hm.'' Marcus had once had a patient who refused an artificial leg because he was hoping for his stump to sprout a real replacement. ''Why didn't you try laying on of hands?''

''Don't make fun, Marcus.''

''Mom, if it's what Dad had, the symptoms won't go away.''

''Then what's the point of calling you?''

''That's great!'' He could hardly stand to look at her.

''Well?''

''How about to find out the truth.''

She slumped back in her chair. ''I'm so tired of the truth, Marcus.''

''I'm tired of it, too, Mom. But we've got to find out.''

''I know. What do you want to do?''

''Let me take him back with me.'' Marcus stood up.

''To Wisconsin?'' she asked in amazement.

"Hey, it's up the road a way. It's not like we'd be going to Turkey."

"Every place seems so far away."

"It's real simple, Mom. We'll do a CAT scan and I'll call you."

"You wouldn't frighten him, would you, Marcus?"

"No, I wouldn't, Mother." He bent down and kissed her on the cheek. "Who knows. There's even the possibility that I'll have some good news for you." Christ, he sure hoped so.

David popped a Tina Turner tape on his cassette and adjusted the sound so he could hear a little bit of Tina and a little bit of Vera's sugary voice over the phone. He sat on his bed and leaned back against the wall, tapping his fingers to the music while Vera went on about her afternoon water-skiing, about the party that coming weekend, about all the fun she and David were going to have. "Girls just want to have fun," he muttered while she was still speaking.

"What?" Vera asked.

"Nothing," he said. "Just talking to myself."

After a brief silence she said, "David?"

"Yes?" He drew out the word dramatically. Here it comes, he thought. Well, he was done pussyfooting around. The nice thing about mortal danger was that it made life very clear. When you didn't have much time, you didn't have much time to waste.

"Did you get my pictures?"

"Yes, I got your pictures, Vera." He kept his voice neutral, hoping she'd squirm a little.

"Uh, what'd you think?" She *was* squirming.

"They're nice." He left a little room for doubt.

"Yeah?"

"But I'm a little disappointed, Vera."

"Really?"

"Just a little."

"Uh, if the poses are bad, I have some others."

"It's not that."

"Well, what is it then?" A little hard edge was creeping into her voice.

"It's you and me, Vera."

"What's that got to do with it?"

"I never thought it was true love between the two of us, but I did think it was true sex."

"It was," she said. "You sure seemed to enjoy it at the time."

"I did, I did." He did.

"So what's wrong? I did too."

"Well, it's like now you're telling me it was true but that it wasn't free." There was a soft knock on his door, then Marcus stuck his head in. David motioned him into the room.

"And what's that supposed to mean?" Vera asked.

"Simple," David said. "It means I'm not in the modeling business."

He could feel the heat coming through the phone. "Well, David, I just thought . . ."

"My mother runs the agency," he interrupted. "If you want an interview, you should call her. You're a pretty girl. I don't think you'd . . ." He stopped when he heard the click. He moved the phone away from his ear and looked at it, shaking his head. He hung it up and turned to Marcus. "Nobody understands me," he said.

Marcus nodded. "I guess the bright side is that when your mother runs a modeling agency you can always get a date."

"But you can never get the truth."

Marcus shrugged. "Another quid pro quo from the bright book of life."

David gestured toward the den. "No battle scars?"

"Not yet." Marcus moved over to his bicycle and spun the rear wheel. "Just some initial sparring. Hey, your rear wheel's not true."

"It's better than the front one." David had been planning to do something about it, but hadn't gotten around to it yet.

"Got a spoke wrench?" Marcus was looking at the wheel as though it were a patient.

"Yeah." David bent over and pulled out the wagon from beneath the bed.

"Hey." Marcus pointed at the wagon. "You still got that old thing?"

"Sure." David tossed him the spoke wrench. "Life moves too fast these days. Some things you hang onto."

"Right." Marcus began tightening the spokes. "Then you should take care of your equipment. It'll last longer that way."

"I've hit some bad road in the last few days."

Marcus worked on the bike for a few moments, then said, "So how're you doing these days?" In trying to be casual, his voice was so stiff that David nearly burst out laughing.

Instead, he put on a super-serious tone. "I'm doing just fine, thank you. And how are you doing?"

They both guffawed, Marcus shaking his head. "I guess I'm doing okay," Marcus said.

"How's the old Hippocratic oath holding up in 1980s America?"

"I don't bend it any more than is necessary."

"Glad to hear it."

"Speaking of that," Marcus said, "I hear you dropped out of pre-med." He tightened another spoke.

"Yeah," David said. "But the quid pro quo is that I also dropped out of pre-law." He smiled as though he had accomplished something momentous.

"So what're you studying now?"

"Double major," David said. "Eastern philosophy and cowboy movies."

"Sounds heavy."

"It is. The yin and the yang and the bang-bang. I passed up a great double bill to see you tonight."

"I hope it's worth it."

"The night's young," David said.

"You had great SAT scores," Marcus said. "A scholarship. Straight A's your first semester. You . . ."

David felt his hackles rising, and suddenly interrupted his brother. "It's like the stock market, you know. My IQ suddenly dropped forty points in heavy trading, and I woke up the next morning feeling real stupid."

Marcus didn't even smile. "Hey, you mind if we get serious for a while?"

"Sort of."

"Come on," Marcus said.

"You come on. What're you trying to do, be a One-Minute-Brother?"

"I don't think so."

"Well, it sure seems like it. I mean, after a year and a half of phony phone calls you finally show up, late for dinner, and now you want to hassle me."

"I'm concerned about you."

"Hey, if you're still concerned tomorrow you can hassle me then."

"I have to go back to Wisconsin tomorrow."

"That's great!" David looked at him in disbelief. "Why the hell did you bother coming?"

"'Cause I missed you." Marcus smiled warmly at his little brother. "And I'm sorry if it seems like I'm hassling you." He turned back to the bike and spun the wheel. "There. It spins true now."

"Thanks. Sorry I got pissed."

"It goes along with being brothers."

David nodded. "Are you really leaving tomorrow?"

"Yup." Marcus pointed at him. "And I want you to come with me."

"Me?"

"Why not?"

"I don't know." He didn't know. And he didn't know why the idea of visiting his brother had never occurred to him.

"Bring your bike," Marcus said. "We'll ride around. It's been awhile, you know?"

"It has." The idea of riding with Marcus was the best one he'd heard all day.

"How about it?" Marcus asked. "My van's right outside."

"I'd love to," David said.

"Great. We'll leave . . ."

"But I don't think I should leave Mom all alone."

"She's a grownup, Davey. I think she can take care of herself."

"I don't know."

"She might even enjoy not having to cook for you every night."

David shook his head tentatively.

"Davey, I spoke to her. She thinks it's a great idea."

"You sure?"

Marcus gestured toward the doorway. "Ask her yourself."

"I will." David got up and started out of the room. "Either you drugged her senseless or you might be up for the Nobel Peace Prize. Wisconsin. Amazing." He bolted past his smiling brother and ran to the den for his mother's blessing.

3

They left the next morning, David's bicycle locked in the rack on the top of Marcus's van, and a small bag of his belongings in the back. He had no idea how long he would be staying, and he didn't know what to take. A few changes of clothes, his extra bike stuff. Maybe he'd even end up riding his bike home from Wisconsin—he could probably do it in three days if he really pushed himself. Then again, maybe he would die in Wisconsin and not even have to worry about getting home. The thought was a strange one, and even though he knew that his death at any time was a distinct possibility, he couldn't quite take it seriously; there was an unreal side to it—he was alive, after all—and however much he got depressed about the thought of dying, he could never quite imagine himself dead.

His mother had seemed fine about his going, although her hug good-bye was a little too clingy, as though she too feared that it was the last time they would see each other.

You could really drive yourself nuts with this stuff, David thought. He guessed that if he did start having bad symptoms he could get home fast enough. His father's agony had been prolonged. David shuddered at the thought of it. He didn't know which was worse, actually dying or the pain that went before.

"You all right?" Marcus asked. They had just finished dinner and were on the home stretch to the town where Marcus lived and worked.

"Just thinking about how cold it must get up here during the winter," David lied.

"It gets down there."

David had done a lot of dozing on the ride up, and a lot of staring out the window at the passing countryside, saying nothing. He and Marcus had studiously avoided any mention of their father, and aside from a little talk about David's future (which David had cooled out by promising to give the professions another look when school started in the fall), they hadn't said much. David had promised Marcus that he would go to the library and look in to a school away from home that he could transfer to.

"Must be tough riding in that cold," David said.

"Some days you don't go out. But they've got great training facilities on campus. Sometimes I work harder on the machines."

"I'll bet."

"Mom says you've been riding the bike a lot."

"Not much." David grinned. "Only about a hundred miles a day." He almost felt boastful.

"Pretty good."

"So they say."

"Do any racing?" Marcus asked.

David shrugged. "Yeah, sure."

"Really?"

"Well, not really."

"Oh."

"But I do race, uh, *un*really."

Marcus glanced at him, stroking his chin. "Sounds positively metaphysical."

"I go on these long rides by myself, and I sort of pretend I'm in a race."

"Sounds exciting."

"It is." David warmed to his subject. "I'm trying to get away, and these guys are chasing me. They catch me and then we sprint. It makes the miles go faster."

Marcus laughed.

"Does that sound nuts?" David asked.

"Not at all. I do it all the time."

"Do you always win?"

"Never fails." Marcus looked over at him. "You ever race against me?"

David smiled sheepishly. "Sure."

"Really?"

"We had a good one last week."

"How'd I do?" Marcus asked.

"You were pretty good," David said, "but I nipped you at the finish line."

"Son of a bitch."

"You old folks have to step aside sometime."

"Sorry I missed it," Marcus said.

In truth, David knew that he probably could never come close to his brother. "Are you going to try out for the Olympic team again?"

Marcus shook his head. "I'm getting a little too old for that."

"At least you made the team once."

"Really?" There was an edge in Marcus's voice.

"Yeah."

"That's funny," Marcus said sarcastically. "I thought I was an alternate."

"Well, it's almost the same thing." David gestured as though there was no distinction. In his young, idolatrous eyes, his brother *had* made the team. "I bet you could've . . ."

"No *could've,*" Marcus said decisively. "The fact is that I didn't make the team."

"You were damn good. Don't deny it."

"I don't," Marcus said. "But there are decisive moments in bicycle racing, and when that moment came, I gave up."

David looked at his brother as though he were a stranger. He had never heard him talk like this. "No, you didn't."

Marcus made a turn onto a small street, then gave David a knowing look. "I didn't, huh? Someday I'll let you in on the secret." He pulled the van over to the curb and stopped. "But now it's time to survey my mansion." He killed the engine and turned off the lights.

"That yours?" David pointed out the window on the passenger side to a little wood-frame white bungalow.

"Needs a paint job, doesn't it?"

"I didn't say anything."

"You didn't have to. Come on, let's go inside."

"Sure." David opened the door and stepped out on the sidewalk, stretching his cramped legs. The porch light was on, but the rest of the house was dark. "I thought you doctors were all millionaires."

Marcus laughed. "Those are the guys doing breast implants. I'm just doing research on athletes."

"Such purity," David said, hiding his admiration.

"As driven snow. Come on. Let's get this bike down."

They unloaded the bike together, David taking a few moments to wipe off some of the larger bugs that had splattered against the tires and frame. Then the Sommers brothers walked wearily up to the house.

"Here it is." Marcus opened the door, walked over to a table, and turned on a lamp. He went across the room and flicked on another lamp, bathing the room in soft, warm light.

"Nice," David said. The room somehow reminded him of his dad's study. There was a certain warmth to it, despite the mess. David felt comfortable immediately. Three bikes hung from the walls on hooks. There was a bunch of spare tires, and the mantle was littered with racing trophies.

"You want dessert or something?" Marcus asked.

"No, thanks."

"You sure?"

David nodded. "I'm just sleepy."

Marcus pointed across the room. "You like the look of that sofa?"

"Looks fine to me."

"It's all yours."

"Thanks." David looked around the room once more. "Marcus?"

"Yeah?"

"This doesn't really look like a doctor's house, you know that?"

"I don't. What's a doctor's house supposed to look like?"

"I'm not sure. But whenever the newspapers wrote about 'bombed-out Beirut,' this is what I imagine it looked like."

Marcus grinned, shaking his head. "Thanks, buddy."

David slid off his pants and dropped them by the coffee table while Marcus pulled some sheets, blankets, and a pillow out of a closet. David yawned loudly, and the bedroom door opened as though the yawn had been a cue. A beautiful raven-haired, brown-skinned girl appeared, dressed scantily in white. David shook his head as though he were trying to wake up, but he resisted an impulse to slap his own face. "Oh, Lord," he muttered. He looked to Marcus, then back to the girl, not having the faintest idea what to say.

"Hi," Marcus said.

"Hi," she said.

"I hope we didn't wake you."

"Hope no more." Her voice was like honey. David took off his hat.

As she walked toward the refrigerator, Marcus said, "Sarah, this is Davey. Davey, Sarah."

She smiled at him. "Hi, David."

He cleared his throat. "Nice to meet you." She moved like something he had only imagined. Why hadn't Marcus told him about this part of his life?

She stopped in front of the refrigerator. "Bombed-out Beirut, huh?"

"Sorry," David mumbled.

Sarah brought out a carton of milk and took a long

drink. God, was she lovely! Genuinely, exotically lovely. She put the milk away and leaned against the refrigerator door. "So how do you like Wisconsin?"

"I love it," David said.

"Trip went okay?"

"Uh-huh."

"Davey's a little tired." Marcus walked over and put his arm around Sarah. "We better let him get some shut-eye." He smiled at David. "See you in the morning, Champ."

"Yeah," he said.

"Nice to have you here," Sarah said.

Marcus stopped in front of the door. "Davey?"

"What?" It was an effort to take his eyes off Sarah's legs.

"If you hear strange noises coming from the bedroom, don't worry." He tightened his grip on Sarah. "It's just Sarah and I in the grips of a wild sexual frenzy."

David laughed nervously. "Yeah, sure."

Suddenly Sarah looked him straight in the eyes. Dead serious. "You think he's joking?"

David's smile disappeared. He didn't know what to think. "Uh, no, ma'am."

She and Marcus headed into the bedroom, looking over their shoulders to give him a reassuring smile before they closed the door. David just stood there as though he'd been nailed to the floor, waiting for the ecstatic groans of frenzied rutting to begin shaking the foundation of the entire house. The silence was deafening, and after a few moments he walked quietly over to the mantle and looked admiringly at the bike trophies. On the biggest one there was a little gold plaque that read, "MARCUS SOMMERS—1st Place." Still listening for sounds from the bedroom, David lifted the trophy off the mantle, then held it aloft in the manner of other winners he had seen on television and in the movies. He caught a glance of himself in the mirror, and after feeling momentarily like a fool, decided it wasn't such a bad picture. One of these days he was going to have to get out there and test himself in the real world of racing. If he hung on long enough.

David tiptoed across the room, stopping by the bedroom door to listen—no sounds of combat—then he continued over to the fridge and took out the carton of milk from which Sarah had been drinking. David drank, trying to imagine what her lips must taste like, then a poster on the wall caught his eye. One of the corners had come unglued, hanging over and obscuring the faces of two bike riders going up a mountain. David put the milk carton away and pushed the corner of the poster back to its proper position. Marcus was trailing another racer—it looked like the famous Barry Muzzin—by a couple of feet. Beneath a pale blue sky, both men were grimacing with the agony of effort. Must have been the Hell of the West race David had read about. He look worshipfully at his brother. He was great, no doubt about it. No wonder he had such a fine woman. What a fantastic life he must have, David thought. Doing the kind of work he wants, riding his bike every day, and then to come home to Sarah. What more could you ask for? Probably never been sick a day in his life, either.

David went over to the couch, made up a little bed, and flopped down on it. Maybe he would start racing soon. What did he have to lose? When he had begun to train on his bicycle, it had been without a goal. He liked riding, it passed the time, and it kept him in good shape. He guessed that the psychologists would say that he was simply afraid of competition with his brother, and that was why his races all took place in the safe and magic kingdom of fantasy. If he didn't race for real, he didn't have to worry about losing. Maybe it was true. He guessed that he'd have to try. He had been thinking more and more about racing lately, and although he never timed himself, he thought that both his endurance and speed were pretty good. "One of these days," he muttered. "One of these days." He turned off the lights and snuggled beneath the blankets, wishing that someone like Sarah was there to snuggle with.

4

Sarah took a last sip of coffee and clipped back an errant strand of hair, smiling through the back window at David and Marcus who were busy setting up their bikes. She knew how much David meant to Marcus, and it gave her a warm glow to see the brothers together at last, just like a couple of kids getting ready to head out for a day's frolicsome mischief-making. She shook her head as the sadness began to creep in. Poor David! Marcus had told her about his fears last night, fears they both hoped were unfounded. She tried hard to be realistic, to hold back her emotions until something had been determined one way or the other. No sense in her adding to the anxiety. She grabbed her purse and strode out the back door.

"Morning," she said, smiling at David. She thought it was funny the way he gaped at her like a schoolboy. She looked good. She knew it.

David pointed at her white uniform. "Are you a nurse?"

She shook her head. "Physical therapist."

"Oh."

"She likes to squeeze all those big, muscular athletes," Marcus said.

David stroked his thigh. "I think I feel a deep muscle pull."

She pulled out her car keys. "A good long ride ought to straighten you right out."

David nodded. "I figured you were going to say something like that."

"Where you guys going today?" she asked.

Marcus pulled on his helmet. "I thought we'd go do a few sprints with Eddy."

Sarah shook her head and looked at David. "Be careful, David."

"What's the matter?"

"Eddy's a real son of a bitch."

"Yeah?"

She nodded gravely.

David turned to Marcus. "Who's Eddy?"

"Sarah's right. He's a real son of a bitch."

"Then why are we going to ride with him?"

"He's a good sprinter." Marcus tightened his chin strap. "I need to work on my sprints. I've got a big race coming up."

David shrugged. "Lead me to him."

"See you later," Sarah said. "If you make it back." She gave them a little wave, jumped in her old trusty Dodge and headed for campus.

She worked at the Jackie Robinson Sports Training Institute at Wisconsin State University. The Institute was now in its third year and was developing a national reputation as a place where athletes could come and develop a training program perfectly suited to their abilities and needs. The past month they'd even had an East German track coach come to visit. He had left in a mild huff after Marcus had told him that he could train his athletes to perfection without pumping them full of drugs that would ultimately ruin their lives. Sarah loved working at the Institute. She was a sports nut anyway, and over the past year some of the nation's greatest athletes had stopped in for consultations and therapy. Even some professionals were coming around in the off-season. It amazed her how the Institute's programs were able to bring out potential no one knew existed.

"Hi, guys," she said to a trio of humongous defensive linemen who were lounging sleepily on the Institute steps. "I don't see the love of punishment in your eyes this morning."

"I think I need a rubdown, Sarah," Poncher the nose tackle said.

"That's after the workout," she said. "And only if you hurt yourself."

Swirnoff, the right end, doubled over in pain. "I'm

dying,'' he moaned. ''Sarah, I understand you can heal the sick and raise the dead.''

''Next time you're dead, I'll give it a try.'' She waved at them and went into the building.

She entered one of the bigger training rooms, pausing for a moment to survey the myriad pieces of exercise equipment, wondering what the archaeologists of the future would make of a place like this. There were a few jocks in the room, most of them just sitting there or stretching, waiting for their bodies to wake up. Kushner, the female tennis ace, was using some pulleys with light weights. She raised her head to Sarah in greeting. ''Go get 'em, Susie,'' Sarah said, holding her fist aloft.

She walked through the room and down a corridor, past Marcus's office, stopping in front of another office with ''DR. DENNIS CONRAD'' stenciled on the door. Nothing like being the bearer of bad tidings, she thought as she knocked.

''I'm not in yet!'' Dennis bellowed.

She opened the door and walked in. ''I didn't think so.''

''Hi, Sarah.'' He was breathing hard and his gray sweatsuit was dark with sweat from his morning run. Dennis Conrad was a big black man who had been an All-American linebacker at Wisconsin State and had gone on to play for the Packers and get a medical degree at the same time. Sarah had great admiration for him. He had come from a large, poor family, and had conquered all manner of adversity to get to where he was today. The Institute was a tribute to his perseverance.

''How was your run?'' she asked.

''Not bad for an old coot. How you doin'?''

''Okay. Marcus came back last night.''

''I thought he was going to stay a few days.'' He pulled off a shoe and sat down at his desk. ''What happened? Another fight with his mother?''

''It's his brother.''

''A fight?''

''I wish,'' she said. ''You know the family history.''

''Yeah.'' Dennis wiped his face with a towel and sighed wearily.

''There's a chance his brother's got it now.'' She gave a

little shrug. There didn't seem to be anything else to say or do.

"Oh, Christ." Dennis pounded his fist on the desk. "I mean, that family's got some kind of curse on it."

"I know," she said.

He picked up a pencil and made a couple of doodles. "The brother came back with him?"

"Um-hm. They're out riding now. I think Marcus'll bring him by when they're finished."

"There's nothing to do but check him out."

"David doesn't know that Marcus knows."

"Got the picture." Dennis snapped the pencil in half. "Hell of a way to start the day, Sarah."

"She's amazing," David said. They were coasting down a little hill in the rolling, lush green farm country outside of town.

"I know," Marcus said. "Why do you think I hooked up with her?"

"Where'd you meet her?"

Marcus patted his bicycle. "Riding."

"She's a racer?"

"Just a fan. I met her at a race."

"Maybe I'll start racing."

"Good idea." Marcus hoped he would.

"I mean, she *looks* amazing."

"I think you like her, Davey." They started up another hill.

"What is she, anyway?"

Marcus turned to him and let out a piercing war cry. "Apache!"

"Apache!?" David's eyes opened wide in wonderment. "She's really Apache?"

"That's what I said."

"Jesus!"

"She's also black, Scotch-Irish, and Chinese."

"I've met all of those," David said. "But I've never met an Apache."

Marcus looked at him and shrugged. "I'll tell you,

Davey. There's a whole world waiting for you outside of St. Louis." He bent over and shifted gears. "Now, let's forget about women and work out."

He began to pedal harder, picking up speed. After a few minutes he looked over his shoulder to find David right behind him, not even breathing hard. Not bad, he thought. He stood up and sprinted. He could hear David respond, but after a moment he forgot about him, losing himself in the fury of his sprint, pushing himself farther, farther, and farther. A big race was coming up, and he had to be ready.

Marcus crested the hill with his legs burning and his chest heaving. He relaxed, nodding to himself. It had been a good sprint. He took a deep breath, then looked over his shoulder, expecting to find David many yards behind him.

His little brother was only two bicycle lengths away. He was straining hard, but when he caught Marcus looking at him, he immediately tried to mask his effort. "You don't ride too badly for an old geezer," David croaked, then sucked in a giant breath.

"I think you *have* been training a little bit," Marcus said. "You warmed up yet?"

"Warmed up?" David seemed genuinely shocked by the question.

"Yeah. You gotta be warmed up when we meet Eddy."

"I forgot about him," David groaned. "Where the hell does he live, anyway, Minnesota?"

"Nope. He lives right in that house up there." He pointed to the farmhouse about a quarter-mile down the road, took another deep breath and began to speed up.

"Oh, man," David complained, but Marcus could feel him start to move.

Marcus let out a piercing whistle. "Hey, Eddy!" he bellowed, then whistled again. He speeded up a little more.

"Hey!" David yelled.

"What?"

"We gonna stop, or what?"

Marcus looked over his shoulder and smiled. "He'll catch up to us, believe me."

As he passed the dirt road coming down from the house,

Marcus glanced up and saw Eddy barreling full-speed toward the highway. They had met dozens of times, but Marcus still thought that Eddy was the meanest-looking dog he'd ever seen. "Here he comes, Davey!"

"Christ!" David hollered. "That's Eddy?"

"That's him."

Eddy let go with a vengeful growl in affirmation of his menacing bulldog identity.

"Son of a bitch!"

"Told you," Marcus yelled. "Let's ride!" He slammed into the highest gear, stood up, and sprinted as though his life depended on it, taking a quick look over his shoulder to see Davey following his example. He didn't want to take any chances where Eddy was concerned.

He heard Davey's bike shift, heard his exertion as he strove to distance himself from Eddy's furious jaws. Marcus pumped harder himself, then hesitated for an instant as the loveliness of the scene seemed to freeze in his mind—to the right of him the cornstalks gleaming in the brilliant sun, to the left a herd of Guernseys grazing in a pasture, watched by a pair of red-winged blackbirds perched on a barbed-wire fence. And himself and his brother, pushing their bodies beyond the limit to escape a howling dog. He let out a whoop of joy and pedaled on, feeling as if he could go forever.

Marcus sprinted flat-out for a mile or so, then glanced back to see his brother close behind him. The look on Davey's face said that he was enjoying this too. The doctor was impressed; he had no idea that his little brother was this good.

Eddy seemed to catch the spirit as well, reaching into his bag of tricks like an athlete of true character and coming up with the right stuff for a sudden surge.

"Look out!" Marcus yelled over his shoulder.

Too little, too late. Eddy dove like a wide receiver lunging for a hopelessly overthrown pass, and caught David's right shoe in his frothing mouth.

"Shit!" Davey howled, swinging both legs free from his pedals and struggling to compensate for Eddy's weight so he wouldn't topple to the pavement.

"You all right?" Marcus stopped pedaling.

David flashed him a look of fear before letting go with a laugh. "Would you look at this? The Wisconsin piranha."

Marcus coasted, guffawing at the spectacle of the growling beast wrestling for the trophy of David's shoe. Suddenly the shoe came off, and David nearly capsized again, but managed to pull himself upright and wobble to a stop next to Marcus.

"You're right," David said.

Marcus clapped him on the back. "I am?"

"Eddy's a son of a bitch. Literally."

"Maybe we'll meet his mom on the way back."

The brothers watched as Eddy went for the jugular of the shoe. The brute gnawed and growled, then heaved the shoe into the weeds at the side of the road. For a moment he just stood there, malevolently regarding the brothers, then he tossed his head in disdain before giving chase to a slow-moving produce truck rattling down the road in the direction of his home.

Eddy crested the hill and dipped out of sight, leaving the brothers to look at each other and wonder.

"You think the coast is clear to retrieve your shoe?" Marcus asked.

David nodded. "If it hasn't died of rabies." They began to pedal back. "You can't get that stuff from touching it, can you?"

Marcus laughed. "Just don't put your fingers in your mouth." He held David's bike while he got down and put the shoe back on.

"He always this fast?" David asked.

"He's never caught me," Marcus said. "He must've gotten fired up over the thought of some new meat."

"Thanks."

"Really." They saddled up and started down the road again. "I've never gone that fast before."

"You're shittin' me," David said.

"Not down that road, anyway. You're not a bad sprinter."

David looked at him for a moment, uncertain about believing him or not.

"Really," Marcus said, as sincerely as he could.

David smiled gratefully. "Thanks."

"Now let's see if you can keep it up." Marcus cut loose with a laugh, then took off like a bat out of hell.

They rode for hours, sprinting and cruising along the blacktop highways until David thought they had been to Minnesota and then some. At times he became so fatigued that he seemed to separate from himself, becoming two Davids, one floating along on a magic carpet watching the other grunt and sweat on a ridiculous two-wheeled machine. He could remember riding this hard only a couple of times, days when he was filled with a strange energy or an insistent rage at the face of death which occasionally haunted his dreams.

Today he felt great, although he knew he couldn't have gone so far at such a pace were it not for his need to impress his brother. He knew he had surprised Marcus with his speed and durability, the nod of approval as they coasted back into town meaning more than he could say. David smiled back, then turned away and casually wiped some sweat off his chin. "You do this every day?"

"Most days," Marcus said. "I work on different things different days."

"This was probably a light one, huh?" He still couldn't believe that he had stayed with Marcus through a heavy workout.

Marcus shook his head and spat. "I think you know better than that."

David followed his brother onto the campus, weaving slowly along the paths until they stopped in front of the Jackie Robinson Sports Training Institute.

"This is the office," Marcus said.

David nodded. "Not bad." He watched a pair of tall, lovely co-eds come out of the building and walk across the grass.

"Swimmers," Marcus said.

David shrugged. "I've got nothing against swimmers."

"Come on." Marcus dismounted.

David wearily got off his bike and followed Marcus inside. The quiet Wisconsin afternoon was suddenly shattered by all manner of mechanical noises. "Jesus!" David leaned his bike against the wall next to Marcus's. "Jane Fonda would love this place."

"I don't think she uses machines," Marcus said.

David stared into the giant room. "The industrial revolution comes to athletics."

"I want you to meet someone," Marcus said. "Take a look around while I go find him."

"You sure these machines won't eat me?" There must have been fifty different pieces of apparatus, each one occupied by a sweating, screaming, snorting, or grunting athlete of either sex. There was enough energy being released in the room to generate the power of Boulder Dam. David moved through the room, keeping close to the wall. This place was dangerous.

He stopped by the treadmill, intrigued by the shapely legs of the brunette who seemed literally to be going nowhere fast. An oxygen mask covered her face, and there must have been eight or ten electrodes attached to her body. A couple of staff members and a few other athletes were urging her on. A digital clock next to the treadmill indicated that she had been at it for more than fifteen minutes. Her legs glistened with sweat. David's hand involuntarily reached for his own aching thigh. He knew she was hurting. No pain, no gain, he thought—a second before one of the athletes bellowed the same words at the girl.

David moved a little further down the wall, then stopped to look into another room. Instantly he felt envious of the burly jock sprawled on a training table while Sarah massaged his shoulder. She looked cool and professional, totally in control. David stared at her for a moment, but when she looked up he immediately turned his eyes to the pretty young trainee who stood at her side. He smiled, then looked at Sarah. Sarah tossed her head in greeting, then looked at her trainee. The girl looked up at Sarah who nodded toward the door. This was getting too confusing. Someone poked him in the back.

"Davey?"

He turned around to find Marcus standing there with a large, vaguely familiar-looking black man. "Hi."

"This is Dr. Dennis Conrad, the founder of this place. My brother, Davey."

"Nice to meet you." Dennis extended his hand.

David took it. The hand felt as if it could hurt as well as heal. "Same here." Then it clicked. "Dennis the Menace." David smiled.

"You're too young to remember that," Dennis said.

"Not really. You used to knock some heads around there. I even saw you play against the Cardinals once. My dad took us. Remember, Marcus?"

"Sure do."

"Well," Dennis said, "now I'm trying to knock a little sense into these heads. Of course you've got to have the physical training too."

They began to walk through the maze of athletes straining to the limit with weights, aerobics, rowing machines, Nautilus equipment, and strange contraptions that David had never seen before.

"It's amazing," David said.

"There's a method in our madness," Marcus said. "We try to determine the potential of an athlete and do all we can to help him or her achieve it. We're very scientific. We even use computers."

"We analyze," Dennis said. "And we theorize and proselytize. Sometimes we even sympathize, but we never, never, rationalize." He pointed to the wall. "That's our motto."

David stared at the Latin phrase. "It's all Greek to me," he said.

"*Res firma mitescere nescit,*" Dennis said. "Which, roughly translated, means—" He glanced around the room, then cupped his hands around his mouth and bellowed. "—Once you've got it up, keep it up!" He glanced around the room as several sweating athletes gave him looks of affirmation. "Right?"

"Right!" the athletes responded like a group of soldiers who had just been trained for a dangerous mission.

"All right!" Dennis yelled back. He put his hand on David's shoulder and gave him a warm, friendly smile. "You ready for the torture test?"

"Me?" Maybe they kept a rack in the basement. Or a bed of nails.

"Sure. I love to torture guys your age."

"Uh, I . . ."

"We just finished a hard ride," Marcus said, saving him. "I think he needs some time to rest. Right, David?"

David smiled gratefully at his brother. "Right." He looked at Dennis. "Yes, I do."

"Maybe tomorrow," Marcus said.

"Tomorrow?" He didn't know if he was ready for that, either.

"You free tomorrow?" Dennis asked.

"No," David said. "I mean, yes. Uh, maybe."

Dennis clapped his hands and rubbed them together. "Then tomorrow it is." He slapped David on the back. "See you then, David. It was nice meeting you." Suddenly he turned and stared at the girl on the treadmill. "C'mon, Denise!" he hollered. "You're still alive. Either die or do something!" He began clapping and shouting, urging Denise on. The other athletes picked up the rhythm, gathering around the treadmill as though their combined presence would give Denise superhuman strength.

Marcus folded his arms on his chest and grinned.

"That guy's a real slave driver," David whispered.

"You ought to see him when he's in a bad mood." Marcus patted David on the head. "Maybe he'll be in one tomorrow."

"Thanks for the encouragement."

"After seeing what you did today, I think you can handle anything he can dish out."

"Really?"

Marcus stroked his chin. "Well, *almost* anything."

"I didn't come up here to have a coronary."

"You won't." As he said it, Denise collapsed, and a couple of athletes grabbed her as the treadmill came to a stop.

"Um-hm," David mumbled.

"Tell you what," Marcus said. "As a special treat, I'm going to let you ride home on the bikes with Sarah and help her get dinner ready. I've got a couple of things to do here. Then I'll take a shower and drive her car home."

David grinned. "You trust me?"

Marcus shook his head. "But I trust her."

"I'll try not to poison the salad," David said.

5

David felt very proud riding through town and going shopping with Sarah, watching the longing looks she got from other men and the strange looks that came from older people for whom her dark, exotic looks were obviously too strange. The woman herself was not strange at all. David found her remarkably self-possessed and confident. She seemed to know just what she wanted and was pursuing it with no regrets about what she missed. She seemed centered and calm, qualities David hadn't found in any of the girls he'd met in college, and certainly not in those his mother tried to fix him up with.

After they got back to the house, he took a shower, then joined her in the kitchen and helped her get dinner underway. He set the table and opened the wine, then stood next to her at the counter where he sliced some tomatoes and cucumbers for the salad. As he drew the knife through the vegetables, it dawned on him once again that Sarah was part Apache. He knew that the Indian tribes all had different customs, and he wondered if the Apaches used to scalp their victims. Maybe one of Sarah's ancestors had scalped one of his.

"Sarah?" he said seriously.

"Hm?" She was swaying to the beat of an Eagles album and stirring the beef stroganoff in the pot.

"Can I ask you something?"

She gave him a strange smile. "Does anyone ever say no to that question?"

"I guess not," he said.

She shrugged. "Go ahead."

"Uh, can you speak Apache?"

She laughed. "No."

"Too bad," he said. "Marcus told me your mom was half Apache."

"He told me your mom was half French."

David nodded. "She is."

"Can you speak French?"

"Nope."

She winked at him. "I can."

He heard the front door open and close, and in a moment Marcus walked into the dining room with a familiar-looking girl. "Hello," Marcus said. "Dinner ready?"

"Just about," David said. Something wasn't feeling quite right.

"Davey, this is Leslie." Marcus gestured toward the girl.

"It's *David,*" he snapped, the little boy's name suddenly bothering him.

"Hi, David," she said.

He nodded. "Nice to meet you." He wagged his finger at her. "I saw you, didn't I? I saw you at . . ."

"At the Institute," she interrupted nervously. "I saw you, too." She looked away.

"Well," David said. "Nice to see you again."

"Let's sit down," Marcus said.

"I never expected Dr. Sommers' place to look like this," Leslie said as they walked toward the table.

"You've never been here before?" David hadn't questioned it when Sarah had had him set the table for four. He just figured that the extra place was for a friend of theirs.

"My first time."

"I see." David shook his head and looked at the floor.

"I wonder *who* the occasion is." He pulled out her chair and helped her sit down. As he moved toward his own place he heard Sarah whisper, "Big mistake," to Marcus. "Uh-huh," David muttered, sitting down.

Sarah went to turn off the stereo while Marcus sat down. "Davey's taking our famous torture test tomorrow." The conversational ball was out and rolling.

"Oh, really," Leslie said eagerly.

"Yeah." David unfolded his napkin and put it in his lap. "And I have a feeling you're taking yours tonight, Leslie."

She looked at him in surprise, then dropped her fork, laughing nervously. David picked it up and handed it to her. "Thanks," she said.

"My pleasure." He heard Sarah take a deep breath from the counter where she was shaking the salad dressing. He smiled at her. Maybe he shouldn't feel so negative, but at least they could have checked with him before trying to arrange some romance. He said nothing as Sarah came to the table and sat down.

Leslie dressed her salad and prepared to take a bite. "Dr. Sommers tells me you're into Eastern philosophy," she said.

"Yes," David said. "I'm sure Dr. Sommers told you that." He flashed a cold glance at his brother, then looked back at Leslie. "And when Dr. Sommers tells you to come over to his house to meet his brother who's into Eastern philosophy, you really don't have much choice, do you?"

Leslie dropped her fork again.

Marcus shook his head. "I think you're being very inconsiderate, Davey."

"My name is David, and I don't think I'm being inconsiderate at all!"

Leslie started to stand up. "Maybe I better . . ."

"It's all right," Marcus interrupted. "Don't mind him. Sit down and eat your dinner."

She sat back down.

"You don't have to take orders from him, Leslie," David said.

She shrugged. "I . . ." She stopped, not knowing what to say.

"You can tell him to go to hell." David laughed and pointed to himself. "You can tell *me* to go to hell."

She shook her head. "I didn't come here to tell . . ."

David put his hand on her shoulder and interrupted. "I know how you feel. You seem like a real nice girl, Leslie." He glared at Marcus. "It's just that for once I'd like to meet some girl who doesn't know my mother or my brother." He turned back to Leslie and gave her a friendly smile. Maybe he was being a little too rough.

"The world's full of them," Marcus said sarcastically. "But if you want to find them, you have to leave home first."

"That's great!" David felt furious. "Dr. Considerate speaks. Father dies and you take off the same day. What was I supposed to do? Huh?"

The conversational ball seemed to crash into the middle of the table as though it were made of lead.

"Great," Marcus muttered, shaking his head in disbelief. He looked at David. "This isn't the time to bring up family problems, David."

Leslie started to get up again. "I think maybe I better . . ."

"It's all right, Leslie." David put his hand on her shoulder and forced her back into the chair. "I'm not ashamed of my family. You probably have a mother yourself."

"I do," she said faintly, staring at her lap.

"Well?" David said. "You wouldn't turn your back on her in a crisis, would you?"

Leslie looked at him sadly. She seemed about to speak, but Marcus got there first.

"She created the goddamn crisis!"

"I don't care who created it!" David yelled. "She was crazy about you. Always bragging about her brilliant son. Everything you did . . ."

"I know!" Marcus waved his hand in dismissal. "I know." His voice was full of disgust. "Everything I did was great. When I lost she convinced me I could've won. That there was no difference between the two."

"I don't think that's so terrible," David said. "Do you, Leslie?"

She looked at him, her eyes glistening with tears. "I . . ."

"*I* think it's terrible!" Marcus yelled.

David snorted with contempt. "A lot of people would call it support."

"Father needed support when he was dying!" Marcus shot back. "So where was she?"

Sarah reached out and touched his shoulder as though she were asking him to stop. He flung her arm away and glared at David.

He had no answer. He stared at Marcus helplessly for a moment, then dropped his head.

"Where the hell was she, David?" Marcus demanded.

Sarah reached out and touched Leslie's arm. "Maybe you'd better leave, Leslie."

But Leslie waved her away, shaking her head. She looked at David, waiting for his answer.

He turned back to Marcus. "You know where she was. She was right there in the apartment."

"Yeah," Marcus sneered. "Hiding out in the guest room."

"She fell apart, Marcus! People do."

Marcus shook his head as though there were no explanation for his mother's behavior. "You were there," he said. "You heard Dad calling to her at night."

David nodded, flinching involuntarily at the recollection of those horrible days.

Marcus pointed to himself. "And I had to plead with her to go to him." It was obvious that he had nothing but contempt for his mother.

"Tell me something, Dr. Sommers," David said. "When people aren't as strong as you'd like them to be and they let you down, have you ever considered forgiving them?" He stared coldly at Marcus for a moment, and when it became obvious that he wasn't going to respond, David stood up. To hell with this stuff. He was leaving.

"Oh, God!" Leslie wailed, suddenly dissolving into a blubbering mess. She covered her face and her whole body shook with sobs. The others looked at each other, then they all moved to comfort her.

"I'm sorry, Leslie." David put his arm around her. "It's all right. Come on. I'll take you home."

Marcus stood up and started around the table. "I brought her. I'll take her home."

Sarah shook her head. "This whole thing was my idea! *I'll* take her home."

"No!" Leslie blubbered, standing up. "I'm going home myself." Once again her body trembled with sobs. "Oh, God!" She picked up her purse and started across the room. "I've got to call my mother." Still weeping, she stumbled out the door and into the night.

"Great!" Sarah shook her head at David and Marcus as though they were a pair of rowdy schoolboys whose pranks had just brought someone to grief. She went after Leslie.

David stared at the floor for a moment, trying to shake off the discomfort, then looked back up at Marcus. His older brother returned to his place and took a sip of wine. "You never answered my question, Marcus."

Marcus wiped his mouth with the back of his hand. "I don't have to answer your damn question, but the truth is, yes. I've considered forgiving Mother many times. And I almost did, many times."

David shook his head. "Almost is not good enough."

"Why the hell not?!" Marcus took another drink. "Almost is good enough for everything else in our family. Isn't it?"

David started to respond, but stopped. "Don't wait up for me," he said, then turned on his heel and strode out the door.

He wandered around town for a while, stopping at Lepper's Café where he ate a couple of cheeseburgers while the proprietor delivered a lengthy monologue on his baseball card collection, then walked for another two hours, his fury unabated. He was sorry for whatever he had done to ruin Sarah's dinner, but even she had admitted that it had been her idea to invite Leslie in the first place. How that had led to a discussion about his father's death was beyond him, but he guessed that his resentment over Marcus leaving was always pretty close to the surface. Maybe their mother hadn't handled things very well. But Marcus was a doctor; he was mature, in control, and he should have known about weakness and how to deal with it. David sure as hell hadn't known what to do. He had just started college, and his mind was all over the place. He had been scared silly by his father's illness and death, and his mother's fragility. Marcus's hostile reaction to it had him totally confused. After Marcus left, David had been so busy looking after his mom that he had never had time to properly grieve for his father. God, families! he thought as he approached the house after ten o'clock. They really knew how to do it to each other. He crept up on the porch and looked through the window. The light in the living room was on, but the room was empty and the bedroom door was closed. He tiptoed in and lay down on the couch. There was no conciliatory note from his brother. Big surprise. Marcus wasn't exactly the type of guy that made peace easily. David didn't know what he'd do the next day. Maybe he'd just get on his bike and head back to St. Louis.

He fell asleep and dreamed that he was riding his bike at a blinding speed down an incredibly steep hill. At the bottom a cold white sheet had been raised like the curtain of a stage, and he was going to go through it at sixty miles an hour without the faintest idea about what was on the other side. He sat up with a jerk.

"Sorry," Sarah said. She had just dropped a metal bowl on the floor.

"Um," he grunted. Morning already. Marcus was sitting at the table eating a bowl of cereal. He barely nodded at David. David barely nodded back. He went to the bathroom and got cleaned up, then had a quick bite in silence before leaving with Marcus and Sarah for the Institute.

Sarah seemed unconcerned as she cruised through town, but the tension between the brothers was electric. David still felt angry with Marcus, felt that it was his older brother's place to break the ice and make amends. David was sitting by the window, and as the car went around a curve, the centrifugal force pushed Marcus against him. David didn't even want to touch him, and felt himself scrunching into the door as hard as he could.

When they got to the Institute, he followed Marcus over to the treadmill, doing what he was told to do, but saying nothing in return. He gave Leslie a wave as she walked past. She nodded nervously but didn't stop to talk. As the room began coming to life with exercising athletes, an assistant attached several electrodes to David's body while Marcus and Dennis Conrad conferred briefly on the test. David didn't even give a damn what it was about, and for a moment he felt like ripping off the electrodes and walking out. But what the hell? He'd go through it. He felt so much angry energy that he figured he could do better than Marcus had done.

Their conference finished, Marcus leaned back against a railing while Dennis came over to David and slapped him on the back. "All set, hotshot?"

"Let's do it," David said.

"No questions?"

David shrugged. "All I got to do is put one foot in front of the other, right?"

Dennis nodded. "Just don't try to chew gum at the same time."

"Okay."

Dennis gestured at the machine. "This baby's all computerized. The speed will increase and the grade will increase. You'll go into oxygen debt, and if you last long enough, you'll go into oxygen bankruptcy. Don't worry about it."

"I won't." David took a look at his brother. "I just want to go one second longer than Marcus."

Marcus smiled and stroked his mustache.

Dennis looked at the brothers and smiled. "A little friendly rivalry here, huh?"

"Just rivalry," David said.

There was a blackboard standing next to the digital clock, and Dennis walked over and wrote "25 minutes, 14 seconds" on the board. "That's how long your brother went," he said. "It's a long time, believe me."

"Let's go," David said coolly.

"Here's your mask," Dennis said, handing the oxygen mask to him. "Have a good trip."

David slid the mask over his face while staring at Marcus, then he grasped the rails on either side of the treadmill and locked his eyes on the digital clock. An ominous humming sound came up, then suddenly the mill began to move. David stumbled, then began to walk. A second ticked off, two, three, four. He took his eyes off the clock. The time would probably go faster if he didn't watch. So far it was simple. An easy little stroll. He knew it was going to get tougher. Much tougher. If Marcus had only lasted twenty-five minutes, this thing must be a killer. David hoped he hadn't appeared too dumb by saying that he wanted to go longer than Marcus. He'd just have to do his best; even if he couldn't beat him, he knew he could come damn close.

The machine began to go a little faster, the grade increasing slightly. Here we go, David thought, glancing to the side. Marcus was gone. David looked over his shoulder and saw him standing by another athlete with Dennis, looking at some pictures. Great, he thought. They didn't even care about him. Well, he'd show *them*. He felt some sweat drop from his chin, and he glanced at the clock. Three minutes. *Maybe* he'd show them. The machine kicked again, and David's walking time was done. Time to run. Uphill, too.

Marcus stole a look over his shoulder, noticing that David had passed the ten minute mark, then turned back to his ministrations on Hoss Burns, the school's star running back who had torn his rotator cuff muscle while arm-wrestling with a female javelin thrower. Once David got past fifteen minutes—or maybe twenty—he'd go over and watch, although he doubted that he could cheer him on. He was still steamed about David's behavior the night before. There was no excuse for him making Leslie feel like crap, and then to bring up all that stuff about their mom and dad. The kid was twenty years old; it was time he learned some manners.

Marcus moved on from Burns to Professor Warde, the Victorian scholar from the English department who had recently turned forty and was in serious training to break three hours in the marathon. But Marcus was only half there as they went over his training schedule for the week. He hated getting tossed back into the swamp of feelings that threatened to drown him whenever he thought about his father's death. It was the loneliness of it that appalled him most, the final loneliness. If you couldn't be there for people at that moment, who could you be there for? Marcus felt that he understood weakness, and most of the time he could overlook it, but if you were somebody's partner you didn't leave him out there by himself to face the worst. Something about what his mother had done *was* unforgivable. He was perfectly willing to have a civil relationship; they could leave the unspeakable part unspoken, but that didn't mean he was going to tell her that what she had done was okay.

Fifteen minutes. Let him sweat, Marcus thought. A couple of jocks had gone over to watch David. Marcus decided to wait until twenty. Judging by yesterday's bike ride, Davey could probably make that pretty easily. Then the tough part would begin. The last five minutes of Marcus's test had felt like it had gone on for a hundred years.

Ignoring David, he conferred with a couple of other athletes, then turned back toward the treadmill when he heard a loud cheer. David had just broken the twenty minute mark, and the crowd of spectators was growing.

"You gonna go watch him?"

He turned to find Sarah standing at his side. "I guess."

"Think he'll beat you?"

Marcus snorted and shrugged, for the first time acknowledging to himself that he didn't want to be surpassed by his little brother. He involuntarily reached out as David stumbled and nearly fell, but David quickly regained his balance and got back into the rhythm.

"Let's go over," Sarah said.

"Yeah, sure." Marcus followed her.

The crowd grew, and the cheering and clapping got more intense, reaching a resounding yell as each minute passed. Twenty-one, twenty-two, twenty-three, twenty-four. Even Dennis was right there, cheering David on. Marcus moved around by the blackboard where his own time was posted. David caught his eye and they exchanged hostile looks, but the sight of Marcus seemed to give David a little more energy. He gritted his teeth and ran on. The grade was over twenty degrees; each of David's legs must have felt like a ton of bricks. He looked like he was going to collapse at any second.

The crowd erupted with a thunderous roar at twenty-five minutes. David stumbled again, seemed about to fall. "No!" Marcus yelled, glancing at the clock, not knowing where the word had come from or why. David grabbed the railings with either hand, pulling himself up and forging on. The crowd was counting, three, four, five, six. Marcus felt a sudden and intense admiration of his brother's effort, also a fear that he might falter now and stop, seconds short of the goal. David's eyes seemed to roll deliriously in his head, unable to focus. "Eight! Nine! Ten!" Nearly washed away by an inexplicable wave of love, Marcus clenched his fist and gave David the warmest, most brotherly smile he had. "Come on, David. Keep it up now!"

"Twelve! Thirteen!"

"Keep it up!" Marcus bellowed.

David tossed his head back and returned Marcus's smile, and the love between them seemed to give him more than the energy he needed.

"Fourteen! Fifteen!"

"All right!" Marcus yelled as the crowd went wild. "All right!" he said again, this time softly, almost to himself. He applauded, feeling triumphant, almost as if he had broken the record himself. Well, he had broken through *some* kind of barrier, that was for sure.

Even through the fog of his fatigue David seemed to pick up on Marcus's joy, and his glistening, sweaty body went on and on and on. Marcus looked at Dennis, then the two doctors quickly checked the monitors to make sure that David was in no danger of hurting himself. Everything was fine. The guy was Superman.

Twenty-six minutes. Twenty-seven. The crowd's ecstasy gradually gave way to silent awe, and by the time David hit the twenty-eight minute mark the only sounds in the cavernous room were the whir of the treadmill and the relentless pounding of David's feet.

Dennis poked Marcus and shook his head. "There's no one left to beat," he whispered. Marcus nodded, looking back at David whose eyes seemed to sparkle at the new bond that had been forged between the brothers. At this point he seemed to be doing it all for Marcus.

Twenty-eight minutes, thirty seconds. David stumbled again, then somehow managed to drag himself upright and run a few more strides. His head drooped, his eyes began to flutter, and Marcus could see his legs turning to spaghetti. "Shut it off!" he yelled, leaping onto the treadmill. As the machine stopped, David collapsed into Marcus's arms. Marcus hugged him for a moment, then slid the oxygen mask off his face. He felt David hug him back with what little strength he had left. "Tired so soon?" Marcus smiled down at him, then looked back at the clock. Twenty-eight minutes, thirty-four seconds. "Not bad, little brother." David managed a little smile as the Institute jocks burst into amazed applause.

David felt so safe and comfortable in his brother's arms that he could have stayed there for hours, but he sat up as he felt his strength returning to save Marcus any embarrassment. He nodded modestly to the many athletes offering their congratulations, then put on his cowboy hat and gave Marcus a cocky smile. "Did I pass?"

Marcus punched him on the shoulder. "B minus, kid. Next time you have to work on your form."

"I felt like a gazelle."

Marcus stood up. "You looked like a pregnant water buffalo."

"That was great, David." Dennis Conrad offered his hand.

David stood up and shook it. "Thanks."

Sarah patted him on the back. "You're pretty strong for a guy who doesn't eat much dinner."

"Sorry about that," he said.

"It's forgotten."

"Let's go," Dennis said, starting for another room.

"Go where?" David asked.

"Another little test," Marcus said.

David groaned, following them. "I didn't volunteer for the iron man triathalon."

"This one's simple." Dennis opened the door to another room.

"All you have to do is lie down." Marcus stepped inside and gestured for David to follow.

He took a couple of steps and stopped, his stomach suddenly going hollow with fear at the sight of the CAT scan machine. "And what's this test?" He knew he didn't sound convincing.

"You know what it is," Marcus said.

"It's a CAT scan," Dennis said, just to make sure.

David nodded slowly, looking at his brother. The combination of exhaustion and glory from his last ordeal had robbed him of any will to resist. "This one's for Mom, right?"

"Right." Marcus gave him a big brother pat on the shoulder.

David shrugged. "All right. I reckon you want me to take this off." He took off his cowboy hat and tossed it on a nearby chair.

"Just lie down and let your mind wander," Dennis said, pointing to the cold slab of a table.

David started forward, his weary legs nearly buckling beneath him, then climbed onto the table and spread out.

"Who knows?" Marcus said. "Maybe we'll even discover that you have a brain."

And what else? David thought. And what else? He heard the others leaving, going to look at the computerized display of the inside of his head. The machine went on with a rumbling more ominous than the treadmill, then began rolling toward him. Let it come, David thought. It's not going to find anything that's not already there. Somehow the thought didn't completely comfort him. "Hey, it's just like *Star Wars* down here," he said. "Warp speed." He closed his eyes and let himself drift.

*   *   *

His eyes opened and stared at the gray ceiling. The silence in the room was so tomblike that he imagined they had found the fatal flaw in his brain and decided to seal him in this room for eternity. He sat up, grabbing the T-shirt that someone had put on his chest. He unfolded it, smiling at the Institute's Latin motto written on the front. He swung his legs over the edge of the table and pulled on the shirt. "Hello?" he said. No response. He walked over to the chair and put on his cowboy hat, then approached the forbidding door. To his surprise, the knob turned, and he stepped out into the hallway. It was empty; no cheering crowds to greet him. He shook his head and smiled at his recent feat on the treadmill. He thought he was going to die after fifteen minutes, and he had gone nearly twice that long. Funny the way things worked out. He had gotten on the treadmill full of hatred for his brother and had come off feeling closer to him than he ever had before. Just goes to show what half an hour of going nowhere can do. He wondered what a Zen master would say about the experience.

He knocked on the door of Marcus's office, got no response, so turned the knob and went inside. It was a real office, with a desk, books and filing cabinets. Marcus's diplomas were hung neatly on the wall. My brother, the doctor, David thought proudly. There was even a picture of Sarah on the desk. David stepped behind a partition that divided the room. One of Marcus's bikes was there, a couple of spare wheels, jerseys, shorts, shoes, and other equipment. Marcus had the discipline, that was for sure. David looked up on the wall to find the same picture that he had at home of Marcus pulling him around in his American Flyer wagon. He reached out and touched it as a wave of emotion prickled his spine.

He froze like a thief as the office door opened, then he heard Dennis Conrad say, "I can't believe you're still going to Colorado."

"I'll go if David wants to go with me," Marcus said.

A file drawer opened and closed. David was about to identify himself, but Marcus kept on talking. "He's always wanted to see the West."

"Maybe so," Dennis said. "But you've got to tell him, Marcus."

David's heart began to pound as though he were in the midst of some strenuous exercise. He was afraid they might hear it.

"I can't," Marcus said. "Not now. Not after what he did today."

"I'm not sure I see the point," Dennis said.

"I just don't want to ruin it for him. I love him too much for that."

The light went out, the door closed, and David listened for a moment and the sounds of the two doctors' retreating footsteps disappeared. Then he leaned back against the wall, staring at the ceiling and shaking his head. It's true, he thought, and then he made himself say the words. "I am going to die." He enunciated perfectly. Weird! The sound was too real to bear, so real that it was almost unreal. "Okay," he muttered. "Okay. No big deal." He leaned against the wall for a few minutes more, making resolutions to deal with this news stoically, then mocking himself for his tough-guy posturings. Well, what the hell were you going to do? He finally chose the stoic approach by default. It would be easier for everyone, himself included, if he didn't talk about it. What were they going to do, start a wake and wait for him to die? He knew the good old emotional roller coaster was ready to ride, so he walked out to the hallway and jumped on board. He certainly had a *little* time left, and he was going to enjoy these days with his brother as much as he could.

He went outside and sat on the low brick wall in front of the Institute, just looking at the people who walked by, the trees, the grass, birds and sky, trying to hold it all in his mind for an instant. He was amazed by the variety of life, and it filled him with alternating feelings of joy and sorrow. This is how it's going to be, he thought.

"Hey!"

He looked up and saw Marcus approaching. "Hi." He managed a smile.

"I've been looking all over the place for you."

He gestured at the sky. "I just needed some fresh air."

"Want to hear the results of your CAT scan?"

David smiled again. "I know the results."

Marcus seemed taken aback. "Who told you?"

"Nobody has to tell me. I'm fine, right?"

"Cocky, aren't you?"

David nodded. Don't get too stoic, he told himself.

Marcus slapped him on the back. "Physically, you're not only fine, you have the cardiovascular system of King Kong's first cousin."

"I want to climb the World Trade Center next."

"But emotionally you're a mess."

"How could you say that about your little brother?"

"Because you've got bullshit in your head and lead in your ass, and anybody who wastes the potential you've got pisses me off."

"We can't all be overachievers," David said. Marcus must be bugging him like this to cover up the truth. "Anyway, Shinto philosophy teaches you to accept life as a seasonal occupation."

Marcus stroked his mustache. "Sounds like bull Shinto to me."

David laughed. "I burned your ass on the treadmill, didn't I?"

Marcus nodded. "You also beat my SAT scores. You're great at taking tests every few years."

You'd think this guy would let up, David thought. "Wisconsin's a great state for you, Marcus."

"Yeah?"

"Yeah. The Badger State."

"I'm just warming up," Marcus said. "Here's the thing, Shinto. There's this bike race in Colorado . . ."

"The Hell of the West," David said casually.

"Right." Marcus gave him a look. "Anyway, this is the last time I'm gonna race in it, and I'd really like to . . ."

"I'd love to," David interrupted.

"What?"

"I'd love to race in it." David shrugged as if there was nothing left to say.

"Give me a break, will you?" Marcus said.

"What do you mean?"

"I'm trying to talk you into it."

"All right." David gave him the stage. "Go ahead."

Marcus cleared his throat. "I had a whole speech prepared. You know, about how we never raced together, about how this might be our one chance. Can't you see it? The Sommers team."

"When do we leave?" David asked.

Marcus eyed him for a long moment, then pulled him to his feet. "We leave in the morning." They began walking toward the parking lot. "After we call Mom."

6

Sarah drove them home, and after cracking some beers, they began organizing for the trip to Colorado. Camping gear and sleeping bags were brought out of closets, food and other necessities were packed, Sarah expertly checked out the bikes and extra equipment they were taking and then began to pack some clothes.

"She's amazing," David said, lounging on the couch.

"You already said that," Marcus said.

"Don't you have a sister?" David asked her.

She smiled and shook her head. "But I've got a brother who boils twenty-year-olds in oil and eats them for dinner."

"Actually," Marcus said, "he teaches statistics at MIT."

"Lots of twenty-year-olds there," Sarah said.

David took a sip of beer and smiled. "I can't believe this." He gestured at all the equipment in the room. "We're taking off just like that."

"We have to," Marcus said.

Sarah nodded. "The race is in ten days. When are you going to shave your legs?"

"That'll be the day," David said.

"Cuts down that wind resistance," she said.

Marcus slipped into the bedroom and closed the door, leaving them to their discussion. He wanted to call their mother without any fanfare. He dialed the number, told the secretary who he was, then leaned back against the wall while he was put on hold. There was a click.

"Marcus?" Her voice was tense as a piano wire.

"Hi, M . . ."

"Marcus," she interrupted, "how is he?"

Maybe he was nothing more to her than a conveyor of information. "He's just fine, Mom."

"He is?" It was as though she didn't believe him.

"Clean as a whistle."

"Really."

"Scout's honor, Mom. Hippocratic oath. All that stuff."

Her breath left her in an immense sigh of relief, then she wept openly.

"He's really fine, Mom," Marcus muttered. He let her cry for a few minutes, then said, "Hey, Mom."

"What?" she blubbered.

"Come on. Enough already."

"I can't help it."

"You're supposed to be celebrating."

"I am celebrating." She sobbed again. "I've been living with it for so long." He listened to her sniffle, then blow her nose. "David's all I have, and the thought that . . ."

Suddenly furious, Marcus cut her off. "I was under the impression that you had two sons."

There was a moment of stunned silence. "Of course I do," she said, more businesslike now. "I didn't mean to . . ."

"I know," Marcus interrupted softly, deciding that he wasn't going to make a scene. "It's easy to forget at times."

"That's not what I was going to say."

He laughed. "This whole conversation is probably not what I was going to say."

"What does that mean?" she asked, suddenly concerned.

"It means . . ." He put his hand on his forehead and took a deep breath.

"Davey's all right, isn't he?"

"Oh, Jesus," he mumbled. He leaned forward and stared at the carpet.

"Marcus?"

"Yes, Mom. David is fine. He sends you his love." There was nothing more to say. He had to get off the phone. "I gotta go, Mom."

"Marcus?"

"Yeah?" What the hell did she want now?

"I hope you understand just how much I love . . ."

"I love him too, Mom. I gotta go. 'Bye." He hung up before she could say anything else. He didn't want to hear it anyway. He shook his head wearily and stood up. He was not going to let this get him down. He had a big race coming up, his brother was going to race with him, and he was going to enjoy the hell out of the next couple of weeks no matter what happened. He opened the door and walked into the living room.

"How was Mom?" David asked.

Marcus looked at him for a moment. "She was real happy, that's how."

"Yeah?"

"Yeah."

"How come you didn't let me say hello?"

"She had a couple of pressing calls."

"But you told her I was fine?"

"No," Marcus said. "I told her you got hit by a bus. What do you think I told her?"

"She was real happy, huh?" David smiled.

"Yeah."

"That's great."

Marcus nodded. "Come on," he said, starting for the front door. "Let's go back over to the Institute."

"What for?" David downed what remained of his beer and stood up.

"I got something I want to show you."

They stopped for dinner on the way, and by the time they got to the Institute it was deserted. Marcus led them through the darkened equipment room into one of the little viewing rooms where the athletes could study themselves on film. Sometimes a dismal lesson, Marcus thought, popping a cassette into a VCR and turning on a large television.

"Hard core?" David asked.

"All the way." Marcus started the tape. As the starting line at Morgul Bismarck came into view, he cut the volume to screen out the announcer's voice and the roar of the crowd. He always felt a little thrill looking at the large pack of riders surging away from the starting line.

"That's gonna be us?" David asked.

"That's it." Marcus watched them for a moment. "There are three stages in this race. This is the first, and this is where the field gets cut in half. If you don't finish in the top half, you go home."

He fast-forwarded to a couple of steep descents that featured him flying down the mountain ahead of the pack. David looked back and gave him a nod of approval. Marcus moved on to another descent, a real hairy one around a curve with crowds yelling and waving.

"Wow!" David said.

"Yeah," Marcus said. "It gets real dangerous up in those mountains. Speed's important, but there's a lot of other things to think about. Strategy, finesse, you name it."

"You just did." David seemed genuinely impressed with the many facets of the race.

"Hm." Marcus rocked back and forth on his feet, almost as if he were racing, as he watched himself go on a long, uphill sprint. His legs ached just thinking about that grade. Muzzin was behind him, moving up, inch by remorseless inch.

"That's the guy on the poster in the kitchen," David said. "Muzzin, isn't it?"

Marcus looked at his little brother. "How do you know about him?"

"I do read about this stuff every once in awhile."

"His name is Barry Muzzin," Marcus said. "He used to be my teammate. And my best friend."

David said nothing, seemingly lost in watching the

sprint. Muzzin came on, almost even with Marcus, talking to him as he closed the gap. Just as he pulled even, Marcus stopped the tape.

"Hey!" David said.

"Muzzin's known affectionately as 'The Cannibal,'" Sarah said.

David looked at her. "You know him?"

She nodded. "I was married to him."

David seemed stunned. He continued to stare at her for a moment, then glanced back at Marcus. Finally he shrugged and directed his eyes to the screen.

Painful though it was, Marcus started the tape again, studying every frame as Muzzin started to go past him. As Muzzin looked at him, he watched his own face lose the slightest bit of intensity. "There!" Marcus said.

"What?" David asked.

"Did you see that?"

"See *what*?" David implored.

Marcus stopped the tape, ran it back, then played it again until it reached the crucial moment. He froze the frame on the screen. "Right there the race is over."

"It is?"

"I quit," Marcus said.

"No, you didn't." The loyal little brother.

"Shows you how good I am at it. Nobody can even tell anymore." He'd been over it a hundred times, but he stared at it again, trying to get it to burn through his conscious mind into his unconscious so that he would not experience this failure again.

He let the tape run, Muzzin blasting past to the finish line, his arms raised ecstatically.

"That's what it looks like when you win," Marcus said. He'd had the feeling a few times himself. The crowd closed in on Muzzin who was clearly savoring his triumph. Marcus was nowhere to be seen. So much for second place. "And this is what it sounds like." He turned up the volume and let the roar of the crowd fill the room. Maybe they were stupid, but it sure sounded good when they were cheering for you. He cut the sound and ejected the tape. "And that, little brother, is the Hell of the West."

"You really gave up?" David asked.

"Long enough to get myself beaten. Take a lesson." He wasn't that worried about David, especially after watching him on the treadmill today. David's problems would have to do with the mechanics and psychology of racing. Marcus was more worried about himself.

"I got it," David said. "At least I think I do."

"I hope so."

David stood up and rubbed his hands together. "So we leave in the morning?"

"Bright and early," Sarah said.

"Ought to be a pretty drive."

"Drive?" Marcus asked.

"Yeah. You know. The van."

Marcus pointed to Sarah. "She gets the van. We get the bikes."

"The bikes?"

"That's right." Marcus grinned. This was going to be fun.

"You mean . . .?"

"I mean," Marcus said, "that we have a race. And you've got a few things to learn. What better way to learn than when you're seeing the country. The grand old U.S. of A."

"But we're going to Colorado. It must be . . ."

"About a thousand miles," Marcus interrupted.

"But we're taking two-lane roads," Sarah said. "That might make it a little longer."

Marcus spread his palms. "We do a hundred miles a day on the bikes, we should get there right on time."

"Ten days," David moaned.

Sarah laughed. "I'll give you a ride if it looks like we're going to be late."

"I feel tired," David said.

"Then let's go home and get some shuteye." Marcus opened the door and led them out. "Six o'clock comes mighty early."

"I suppose we have to say good-bye to Eddy," David said.

Marcus put his arm around him. "You're going to love it, Davey. I mean, David. I mean, there's Minnesota, Iowa, a little bit of South Dakota."

"Don't forget Nebraska," Sarah said.

"That's right," Marcus said. "And Kansas! Flat country, David. No hills. Get you nice and ready for that Rocky Mountain high."

"Far out!" David said. "If this be Kansas, can the Tour de France be far behind?"

"That's the spirit!" Marcus burst out of the building and gave a little yell. "Make way for the Sommers brothers!" He linked arms with David and Sarah, and they ran, laughing like innocent children, to her car.

David called his mother that night, but she was so effusive about his alleged good health, that he didn't have a chance to tell her about the Sommers brothers' upcoming race. He got off the phone feeling good. Weird, but good. Marcus had obviously done a real snow job on her. What the hell, David thought. It was probably better that she was living in a happy illusion than having to spend the rest of his life worrying about when he was going to die. And Marcus probably thought it was best for his brother that he didn't know he was going to die. Maybe he was right. David had always been a pretty firm believer in facing the hard truth about everything, but now he was beginning to think that the unmalicious lie might have its place in life. Some philosophies taught that everything had its place in life. Who knew? He tried to imagine what he would feel like now if he hadn't overheard Marcus and Dennis Conrad talking in the office. He would still be dying, but he wouldn't know it. He would be under the illusion that he was healthy and bound to stay that way for the foreseeable future. As it was, he was dying and knew it, and still felt pretty good, mainly because his mother didn't know it. Enough, he thought, letting out a little laugh. When the race was over he would call in a logician and a moralist and a psychoanalyst to do an in-depth study of his feelings and the meaning (or meanings) of same. For the moment, he was going to try to enjoy busting his ass to get across America's heartland.

He came out of the bedroom with a big smile on his face.

"What's so funny?" Marcus asked.

"Mom and life," David said.

"In that order?" Sarah asked.

He shrugged. "Depends on the hour of the day." He walked over to the table where Marcus was studying a map. "How's it look, General?"

"I don't want to break your heart, David, but I think we're going to skip Minnesota and South Dakota."

"Aw, shucks."

Marcus pointed at a blue line on the map. "I think we'll cross the river at Dubuque, and if the troops are still strong we'll march on to Maquoketa."

"And doubtless take it by storm," David said. He studied the map for a moment, feeling a rush of excitement as he mentally pronounced the names of towns—Cedar Rapids, Tama, Fort Dodge, Sioux City, Cherokee—and looked at the tiny circles that designated their places in the scheme of things. He was actually going to see these places, blast through them like some pony express rider and disappear into the sunset. A young man, going west. It would probably be his only trip. He resolved to make it a good one.

7

Marcus made it clear on the first day that whatever idyll of the American landscape David was planning to experience would occur when they were riding in the van. When they were on their bikes, they were training—not coasting and pedaling, but hard, fast, and concentrated training. David's speed and endurance were excellent, but Marcus was going to have to teach him how to race in ten days while sharpening his own skills as well. They were going to be up against some of the best racers in the world—Marcus was one of the best himself—racers whose talents were not developed while they were screwing around. This was very serious business.

David surrendered to the task. There was plenty of scenery to see from the van (they were on the bikes four to six hours a day), and after his initial discomfort, the idea of honing himself to perfection became more and more appealing. What the hell else did he have to do anyway? The fact was that he didn't know how long he had to live, and he didn't want to pass up an opportunity to achieve his full potential. He really didn't think that much about winning the race, but the thought of losing because of doing something stupid became more and more repellent to him.

One day, after a light lunch, they left Sarah sitting in a café in Dennison, Iowa, and rode out on Highway 30, heading for the Missouri River. Most of the time they rode side-by-side, David listening while Marcus coached, or simply responding to his older brother's moves. A lot of sprinting, followed by plain hard riding, the trick seeming to lie in how hard you rode, and for how long. Every time David thought he understood the game, Marcus would throw in a new wrinkle. Today Marcus seemed to be doing shorter sprints more often. They had just slowed down, and David was looking at a billboard featuring a pretty girl diving into the swimming pool of an Omaha motel when Marcus took off again.

"Shit!" David muttered, lowering his head and giving chase.

"Head up!" Marcus bellowed.

David raised it.

"Keep your eyes on the road!" There was a note of irritation in Marcus's voice.

"Yeah, yeah," David said under his breath. He knew. Don't watch the road and you'll run into something. Or off the road. He didn't like the little orders Marcus gave him, but he knew they were important. One lapse of concentration could cost you a second. One second could cost you the race.

"Toestraps!" Marcus yelled.

"They're fine."

"Check them!"

David did, lowering his head again. Marcus was gone. Son of a bitch, David thought, pouring it on, finally catching up.

Marcus veered out a little, David following his path. Suddenly he cut back to the inside, and David, who had again dropped his head, ran right over the pothole that Marcus had led him to.

"Head up!" Marcus bellowed. "Head *up*!"

"Nice guy," David muttered, struggling to catch up.

The van cruised slowly past them, Sarah saluting them with a large container that held a cool drink. Marcus didn't wave. David did. Marcus took off.

"Damn!" David yelled, chasing him again. Concentration was everything. He was beginning to think that the mental part of the race was more important than the physical. Would the yin and the yang never desert him?

They sprinted on and off for another fifteen miles, David making a major effort to catch Marcus as they came around a curve. About a mile and a half down the road the van was parked on the shoulder. David gave it everything he had, and he could tell that his older brother was doing the same. But David's anger at being suckered into the pothole seemed to give him an extra edge, and over the next two hundred yards he managed to pull even with Marcus. As David's front wheel inched in front of his older brother's, Marcus flashed him a pooped expression, shook his head, leaned back in the saddle, and began to coast. David felt as if someone had set his thighs on fire, and, grateful for the rest, he leaned back himself.

Then Marcus was gone. Sarah had appeared at the side of the van and was waving a dirty rag as though it were the checkered flag at a race. And Marcus had put twenty yards between himself and David before David could even respond. Still, he managed to process his embarrassment quickly, standing up and sprinting for the van even though he had no chance of catching Marcus.

"He cheated," David yelled as he finally rode past a smiling Sarah.

"You're kidding." She feigned surprise.

Marcus was already making a U-turn and coming back, his arms raised in mock victory.

"I'm not!" David yelled.

Sarah held her hand to her chest. "Not Marcus. I can't believe it."

David made his own U-turn, came back and stopped. He let out a deep breath and shook his head at Marcus.

"That was a good sprint, David."

He spat. "Guess I screwed up, huh?"

"It was a sucker move." Marcus wiped his brow. "They happen all the time."

"They've happened all the time *today*," David said.

"Beware of friendly collaboration in races," Marcus said. "Especially if the friend is on another team. He might be the sweetest guy in the world, but if his jersey is different than yours, the only thing he wants to do is beat you."

"Concentration," David gasped.

Marcus patted him on the back. "That's the bottom line, kid."

"You think I'm gonna be ready?" He was really beginning to doubt himself.

Marcus nodded. "By the time we get halfway across Nebraska you'll probably be leavin' me in the dust."

"That'd be a change."

"Anyway," Marcus shrugged. "Let's rack these things and let Sarah show us the countryside for a while."

"Amen, brother." A grateful David undid his toestraps.

They crossed the Missouri River and entered Nebraska, setting up their camp outside of Blair, within walking distance of the water. They grilled steaks over the coals while roasting potatoes and corn in aluminum foil, and after they had eaten and cleaned up, David took a little walk by himself along the river. He had begun to feel irritated with the facts of life, especially the fact that the race wasn't going to be pure. It seemed to him that the purity of one's talent—his speed and endurance—should be the only thing that mattered, but now Marcus was telling him that there was a cutthroat side to the business as well. It was like a bunch of businessmen sitting down to work out some merger—everybody looking for a weakness so he could screw the other guy. Well, David didn't want to be a part of it. If he was going to beat anybody it would be because he could ride a bicycle better than they could. No tricks. No sucker moves that could hurt the other guy.

He picked a dry stick off the ground and lobbed it out onto the water. It moved slowly away from him, heading south toward Omaha, then to where the Platte River joined the Missouri, then down to St. Joseph and Kansas City before turning east across Missouri to St. Louis. Maybe the stick would float by his mother's condo while he was pedaling up some hill in Colorado. He thought of Li Po, the Chinese poet, who was rumored to write beautiful poems, then crumple them up, throw them on the river and watch them float away. Maybe that's the way David wanted his racing to be—just by himself, with no one else to see it or corrupt it. "Nope," he said, tossing a stone into the water. That wouldn't work. Deep in his bones he knew that he really wanted to get out there and compete. He thought he could do it without turning into a monster. The main thing was to do the best he could; if there were people out there waiting to screw him, he'd just have to be aware of it and watch out for it—he didn't have to do it himself. He guessed that racing must be pretty much like life itself. Shinto philosophy to the rescue once again.

It was dark when he got back to camp, and for a moment he stood outside the light from the campfire, watching Sarah and Marcus. They looked pretty helpless, or at least they would be if they were surrounded by Indians with tomahawks and lances. He thought of letting out a ferocious whoop, but he didn't know how Sarah would take it, so he crept quietly through the underbrush like a cavalry scout returning from a night reconnaissance mission. He slapped a mosquito that was doing something horrible to his neck. A very unscoutlike move.

"Hey," Sarah said, smiling at him. "Where you been?" She was arranging the sleeping bags a few feet away from the fire.

"Pretending I was Kirk Douglas in *The Big Sky*." David pushed his little finger into his chin, trying to make an indentation.

"That was a good one." Marcus didn't look up from the shoe into which he was screwing a new set of cleats. "That's when he pushed all those people across the Oregon Trail or something, wasn't it?"

"No, no." David shook his head and gave Marcus a shame-on-you look. "That's something else. This is the one where his buddy got him drunk so he could chop off his thumb with a hatchet."

"Oh yeah," Marcus said.

"Some buddy," Sarah said.

David shrugged. "Someone had to save him from the gangrene."

"They were always doing that in those movies," Marcus said.

"It was before we had you geniuses of modern medicine," David said.

Marcus smiled at him. "I never invented anything. No new cures from Dr. Sommers."

Sarah reached over and stroked his shoulder. Marcus covered her hand with his.

"Speaking of that," David said.

Marcus tightened another cleat. "Yeah?"

"I was just wondering. Uh, if Dad were alive today..." He trailed off, looking to the stars for help.

"What?" Marcus said.

"Well, they didn't have any cure for a Berry aneurysm two years ago."

"Right." Marcus stared at him.

"I was just..."

"They still don't," Marcus interrupted, turning back to his shoe.

"Nothing?" David asked, more than a little request for hope in his voice.

"Not really."

"But there must be some kind of operation." Maybe it wasn't fair to ask his brother these kinds of questions.

"Won't work," Marcus said.

"Even with all these lasers and microsurgery and stuff like that?"

Marcus took a deep breath and shook his head. "If there's a weak blood vessel and it's located deep inside the brain, you can't get to it without damaging the patient's vital brain functions."

David tried to smile. "Meaning the patient could become a chef's salad."

Marcus looked at Sarah and actually laughed. "That's one way of putting it."

"You'd think they'd invent something," David said.

"Maybe someday," Marcus said. "But not today." His voice didn't leave much room for hope.

David spit out a piece of bark from the twig he'd been chewing. "The thing is, you know, you read all these stories. All of a sudden some bald guy starts growing hair again. Needs a haircut every week."

Involuntarily, Marcus ran his hand through his hair. "I don't think that was in the *New England Journal Of Medicine*."

"But you know what I mean," David said. "People can do a lot of things through will power."

Marcus nodded skeptically.

"What do you think of that stuff?" David asked. He couldn't let it go.

Marcus gave him a big brother smile. "Sounds like Eastern philosophy meets the Hell of the West to me."

No hope. David nodded. "That's what I thought you'd say."

"Tell you what," Marcus said. "You put all that will power of yours into the race and you'll do better than you thought you could.'' He stood up, walked over to a sleeping bag, dropped to his knees, and began taking off his shirt.

''Maybe.''

''No maybe about it,'' Marcus said. ''You've got to believe in yourself, David. A lot of things can happen when you do.'' Marcus slid out of his pants and into his sleeping bag. Sarah lay down beside him.

David chewed on the twig for a moment, watching them, then looked up at the starry sky. Suddenly he cut loose with a piercing coyote howl. When he looked back at Marcus and Sarah, they were both sitting up, staring at him in disbelief. He gave them a little grin. ''I've always wanted to do that.'' He took a deep breath and pounded his chest, suddenly feeling terrific, nearly at one with it all. He tipped the brim of his cowboy hat. ''Good night,'' he said.

8

The thrill was gone. It was. It truly was. Becky Chandler stared at a pothole in the blacktop of Highway 83 and finally admitted to herself that the thrill was gone. Wearily, she looked up and down the highway. Not a vehicle in sight. Her feet were hot and her legs were tired. She wanted a ride. Preferably in an air-conditioned luxury car.

''Hey, we're in Kansas,'' Frank said, forcing a smile. He stroked his beard and stared reverently at a wheat field.

''Far out,'' Becky said. The thrill of crossing state lines was definitely gone.

''Come on, Becky,'' Susan said. ''Think of how far we've come from Ohio.''

''I'm thinking of the 747 that's going to take me back.''

''Weak sister,'' Susan said.

''Whatever.'' Becky thought she heard the sound of a vehicle and looked expectantly back into Nebraska.

"Negativity can slow us down," Frank said.

Becky didn't think so, but said nothing, watching the speck in the distance gradually transform into a van with a couple of bicycles stuck on top. In deference to Frank, she put on a happy face, smiling brightly as the trio lined up and stuck out their thumbs. The dark-haired driver looked friendly enough, but the van cruised past without slowing down. Becky flipped the finger at the van as her hitchhiking smile faded to a scowl.

Frank shook his head disapprovingly.

"What's the matter?" Becky demanded.

"Too many negative vibes."

"Gimme a break." Becky faced Kansas and started to walk.

"Really," Frank said. "Drivers pick it up."

"Like dogs smelling fear on a person," Susan said.

These are the pitfalls of one semester of freshman philosophy, Becky thought, wishing she had taken a second semester. It might have given her the wisdom to stay home for the summer. "Then how come it's the perverts who pick us up when I'm thinking positively?"

Susan and Frank looked at each other for a moment, then Frank raised his hand as though he were in the classroom. "Their vibes are scrambled anyway."

"Frank's right." Susan nodded vigorously. "They can't get a clear picture of people."

"But they know what they like." Becky let out a silly laugh. What a world, she thought. All of these people riding around in vans and trucks and cars, most of them looking just like Mr. Bigelow next door, but with dark sides to them like you wouldn't believe. Well, education had been the purpose of their trip, the trio from Philosophy 6A at Ohio State University who had decided that the "meaning of life" had more importance than Buckeye football, and they were certainly learning *something* on their trek across America. Exactly what it was she didn't know. Maybe she was learning what she liked.

She flipped on her portable radio, but was able to raise nothing but a lot of static and a hillbilly song about how too much whiskey had ruined love, job, and life. She turned off the box and looked back at Frank who was rummaging around in a small carton and feeding his face. "I'm starved," Becky said. "What've you got?" As though she needed to ask.

He extended the carton to her, smiling. A couple of seeds were stuck in his beard.

She shook her head wearily. "I'm tired of granola and sesame seeds." She stopped and framed an imaginary picture with her hands. "I want a chocolate shake and a Quarter Pounder with cheese." She looked at the others and smiled. They forced looks of disapproval, but she knew that their stomachs were probably rumbling just like hers. "And a large order of french fries." Just to rub it in.

"I thought we were going to live off the land," Frank said, his voice quavering with lust for a Quarter Pounder.

"We made a vow," Susan said fiercely. "I plan to keep mine."

Becky pointed to Frank's carton and flashed a sarcastic look. "I don't see how buying generic nuts in a supermarket is living off the land."

"At least it's natural," Frank said.

She stifled an impulse to tell Frank that his love of granola was *un*natural. Instead, she turned on her radio once again, fine-tuning the dial until she finally picked up some soothing rock and roll. She snapped her fingers and did a little dance, then smiled at her morally righteous companions. Something caught her eye, and she pointed behind them. "What the hell is that?' she said, watching the two bicyclists bearing down on them. "The pony express?"

The guy in front had a mustache and was staring intently, straight ahead. He veered off to the side and his younger partner raced ahead, his expression equally serious. They were a weird-looking pair with their shiny black shorts and crash helmets. Racing out of Nebraska. The lead rider gave a quick look at the group, focused on the road again, then suddenly stared at Becky. She smiled, swaying to the music, and gave him a little wave. She thought he began to smile, but then both bikes whizzed past her. "Go get 'em," she muttered, wondering if they'd been riding as far as she'd been walking and hitchhiking. She looked over her shoulder at the departing bicycles and caught the younger rider looking back over his shoulder at her. She understood his not being able to give her a ride.

"Don't even think about it," Marcus gasped.

David nodded, facing front and pedaling on. "Did I really see what I thought I saw?" he yelled. "Or was that just a Kansas mirage?"

"You saw what you thought you saw," Marcus said.

"I didn't think they made mirages like that."

"But don't think about it."

"Why not?"

"Takes off the competitive edge."

"Then why did you bring Sarah along?"

"So I wouldn't get too competitive." Marcus pedaled past David, smiling and giving him a friendly pat on the back.

David's back felt funny and he gave a little wiggle. Friendly pat, my ass, he thought, feeling the banana peel that Marcus had put in the back pocket of his jersey. He said nothing, biding his time for two miles until it was his turn to take the lead. He gave his older brother a friendly smile as he sailed past, then reached for his water bottle. He aimed it to the left of his face—right over his shoulder—and squeezed.

"Son of a bitch!" Marcus spluttered.

"Say what, Bro?"

"You knew."

"I knew?"

"About the banana peel."

David looked over his shoulder and grinned. "My mama didn't raise no dumb children."

"You're learning," Marcus said. Then he stood up and sprinted past him.

The Sommers brothers raced on for ten more miles, David feeling more exhilarated than he had all day. They were more than three-fourths of the way to Colorado now, and he knew he was a lot stronger and maybe a little faster than when he'd left Wisconsin. Most important, he was also more savvy, his mind alert and tuned in to the mechanics and strategy of racing. So he was surprised when his enthusiasm suddenly began to fade. Bingo! All of a sudden it was gone, just like the sun disappearing behind a dark storm cloud. He was leading Marcus up a hill, and he stopped pedaling before he got to the top.

Marcus came alongside and put his hand on David's back, pushing him for a few feet. "Don't worry," he said. "I'm all out of banana peels."

David just looked at him and scowled.

"You all right?" Marcus looked concerned.

"I'm just tired of all this."

Marcus smiled and shrugged. "So what?"

"So what?!" He didn't think his puritanical brother would let such a confession go by so easily. "What do you mean, 'So what?' "

"So you're tired." Marcus pedaled past him. "Big deal. Let's ride."

David was cut off from saying something nasty by a pickup truck with a bad muffler that roared past them. In the back was the trio of hitchhikers they'd passed back by the Nebraska line. The tall blond sexy mirage waved. David tossed his head in greeting as he stood up to sprint. As long as he kept the truck in sight, David was able to race like a champion, but finally it got too far ahead of them, disappearing around a curve, to be seen no more. David tumbled back into the slough of despond and was barely able to summon the energy for a poor showing in the final race to the van. Marcus was already out of his toestraps by the time David stopped. "Sorry," David muttered, sensing his big brother's disapproval.

"What happened?"

"Just the facts, ma'am," David mocked.

Marcus blinked, unamused. "Well?"

"Guess I lost it." David undid his toestraps.

"You lose *it,* you lose the race. Simple math."

"It happens to the best of us." He couldn't resist the dig.

Marcus gave him a look but decided not to respond. They racked their bikes in silence, then climbed into the van, and let Sarah chauffeur them toward Atwood.

It was the girl who had done it, David thought, watching a tractor stir up a small whirlwind in a passing field. It was the girl who had made him think of other girls until he got socked in the face with the fact that he didn't have a girl. He shivered, feeling lonely, and he groaned aloud at the thought of dying lonely. Everything was coming down on him like a ton of bricks.

"What went on back there?" Marcus asked.

David eyed him, unable to speak. He chewed a bit more vigorously on the twig that he'd snapped off a bush on the side of the road.

Marcus shrugged, turning back to the front of the van. "Let me know when you want to talk about it."

"Maybe I made a mistake," David said. "You know?"

Marcus shook his head. "I don't know. Doctors aren't psychic. Neither are brothers."

"Maybe I don't want to race."

"I don't understand that."

"What's the big deal?"

Marcus stared at him, stroking his chin. "The big deal, partner, is that this race means a lot to me."

David nodded. "Fine."

"Fine?"

"Yeah. The race means a lot to you, you race."

Marcus exhaled sharply. "That's great, David. Really great."

"What's the problem?"

Marcus looked at David as though his little brother were an imbecile. "Why do you think I brought you along, you dipstick?"

David smiled. "Because you knew I always wanted to see the West."

"I never said that." Marcus pounded the seat with frustration. "You're the guy that jumped at the chance to race."

"Fine."

"There you go again. What's that, some kind of Shinto answer to everything?"

"It means that now I'm jumping out."

"Can you believe this guy," Marcus said to Sarah. He looked out the front windshield for a long moment, then turned back to his brother. "Look, everyone there is going to have a team. Somebody to draft off. To help them."

"You're good enough to win by yourself."

Marcus shook his head. "I can't win it alone. No one can. I need your help."

"No, you don't."

"You have the endurance, David. I have the speed."

"You hear that, Sarah?" David said.

"What?" she asked coolly.

"Marcus wants to use me."

She looked back at him and smiled. "I'm staying out of this."

David shrugged. No help there. "You're one helluva terrific guy, Marcus." He was beginning to feel angry and frustrated.

"Thanks," Marcus said. "I've always tried to be."

"I mean, you'll use your own brother." He eyed Sarah for a moment, then blurted it out. "You'll steal your teammate's wife. You'll . . ."

"Whoa!" Sarah yelled. She slammed on the brakes, bringing the van to a stop in the heart of downtown Atwood, Kansas. "Hold it right there!" She whirled in the seat and stared fiercely at David.

Never had he known more clearly that he had said the wrong thing. "I . . ."

"He didn't steal me," she interrupted. "I am not a package to be stolen."

"I know," David murmured.

A car behind them honked. Sarah paid it no mind. "I left Muzzin," she said. "I left him because I had to leave. I had to leave because I fell in love with your brother." She paused for a moment to let the information sink in.

David nodded. It had sunk in.

Sarah nodded back. "Thank you," she said. She turned

around and put the van back into gear as another horn honked. "You two may now continue your argument."

David and Marcus stared at each other for several seconds, then they both burst out laughing.

TRAGEDY IN ATWOOD, KANSAS. Becky Chandler could see the headlines now. FRIENDS PART BENEATH THE GOLDEN ARCHES. She waved good-bye to Frank and Susan who half-heartedly returned the gesture from the back of the pickup, then she inhaled deeply, holding in the fumes exuded by McDonald's. She wondered if the sour looks on Frank and Susan's faces were because of disappointment in her or envy over what she was about to eat. Ah, well, she thought. These things happen between friends. They could all patch it up next year in Philosophy 6B—as long as they didn't have to do it over a bowl of granola.

She strode into the restaurant, unsure about everything except her immediate plans. She grabbed a plastic straw out of the container and chewed on it. Maybe she'd get a motel room tonight. Have a real bath and watch television. She stared at the menu for a moment, then shook her head and laughed. She had known exactly what she wanted for the last two days.

"Can I help you?" the attendant drawled.

"Oh, yes," Becky said enthusiastically. "You sure can. I want a Quarter Pounder with cheese, large fries, a chocolate shake and a Diet Coke."

"For here or to go?"

"Here." Might as well get the atmosphere as well as the food.

The attendant checked the stock behind her, then turned back to Becky. "There's gonna be a little wait on those Quarter Pounders. How about a Big Mac?"

Becky shrugged off her disappointment. "Okay." She stared at her knapsack on the floor, feeling as if she had made a big mistake. "Wait a minute."

"Yes?"

"I'll wait for the Quarter Pounder." Another few minutes sure wasn't going to kill her. In fact, the contemplation of the burger would only further enhance the taste.

The laugh had helped to break the tension between David and Marcus, and nothing more had been said beyond Marcus hoping that David would feel differently tomorrow. He didn't know if he would feel differently tomorrow. He didn't know if he would want to ride another hundred miles, busting his ass for something he wasn't quite sure he understood. He wasn't going to push himself. If he felt like it, he felt like it. If he didn't feel like it, maybe he'd just sit in the van and watch the countryside drift by.

Sarah pulled into the McDonald's parking lot, and David got their orders and piled out of the van. Maybe he'd feel better after a good meal. God, he felt miserable. He bit down on his twig and pushed through the door into the restaurant.

"Oh, Lord," he mumbled, thinking briefly that he had gone insane. The mirage was at the counter. Or at least it looked like the mirage. Perhaps it was a mirage of a mirage. An enigma wrapped in a mirror. Perhaps he was stone crazy. Relax, boy, he told himself, pushing his hat back to a more rakish angle. The twig in his mouth was going up and down with every heartbeat. Forward, march, son. You've got dinner to order for three hungry people.

Then he was abreast of her in the next line. She turned. It was the mirage. The plastic straw between her teeth jumped up and down a couple of times. She recognized him. He smiled. They didn't really "know" each other, but they had seen each other and waved to each other. Surely that constituted enough familiarity to say hello. You're going to die, David thought. What do you have to lose?

"Hello," he said.

She gave a nervous wave. "Hi."

"Hi," he replied.

"May I help you, sir?" the attendant asked.

"Yeah." But it was tough to take his eyes off the girl. After a moment he turned away, placed his order, then turned back again. The mirage had not vanished.

She looked at him, grinned, then looked away.

"Uh," he said, "you're eating here?"

"Yeah." She nodded. "You too, huh?"

"Um hm." Keep it rolling, David! he exhorted himself. Keep that old conversational ball rolling along. "Where you headin'?" he asked.

She shrugged. "I don't know. Maybe California."

"Sounds nice."

"How about you?" she asked.

"Colorado."

"I hear that's nice, too," she said.

"So I've been told." He looked around the restaurant. "Where are your friends?"

"We split up."

"Must've been sudden."

She nodded. "We had a major food fight. They don't approve of places like this."

"Too bad."

She shrugged. "At this point I'd just as soon have the Quarter Pounder."

The attendant brought her burger to the counter and set it on a tray. "There you go."

"Thanks." The mirage picked up her tray. She *was* going to vanish. She looked at David for a moment, and for a moment he allowed himself to think that she didn't want to leave. "So what do you do?" she asked. "When you're not riding bicycles."

"That's what I do," he said. The attendant placed a large bag of food in the middle of a cardboard drink container. "Thanks," David said.

"Really?"

"Really. I'm a racer." He felt a sudden pang of guilt. A moment ago he had quit racing. Quit before he had begun.

"I never heard of that." They began moving tentatively away from the counter, the mirage kicking her knapsack as though it were a soccer ball.

"You really never heard of bike racing?" He tried taking little bitty steps.

She shook her head. "Is that what you guys were doing today, racing?"

"Oh, that!" David said as though it were nothing. "That was just training. For this big race in Colorado." The door kept getting closer and closer. His voice became more urgent. "You race up to the top of the Rockies and back. Real dangerous stuff."

"Sounds like it."

He nodded vigorously. "One wrong move and you're just another statistic of the Hell of the West."

"God," she said.

They stopped. The door was next. There was a booth beside it, and it looked like she was going to sit there.

"Well," she said, "I hope you come out of it alive."

He gave a shrug redolent of macho fatalism.

"Good luck," she said.

He nodded. "You too." He leaned against the door without enough force to open it. She started to sit down, but kept looking at him. "Hey?" he said.

"Yeah?"

He shrugged. "How would you like a ride as far as Colorado?"

"Where?" She smiled. "On your handlebars?"

Sarah looked over at Marcus, who was staring sullenly out the front window of the van. "You all right?" she asked. She knew he wasn't, but she didn't want him bottling it up inside and ruining his concentration.

"What's wrong with him, anyway?"

She reached over and stroked his shoulder. "Maybe he's lonely. Maybe he's afraid of racing his big brother."

"He shouldn't be."

"This is all a new experience for him, Marcus. You can't expect him to sort it out right away."

"You'd think he'd be enjoying himself. I don't know." He shook his head.

They sat in silence for a moment, then she said, "It's not right, Marcus."

"What?" He looked at her.

"You should tell him the truth, that's what." Instantly, his face told her that she'd gone too far.

"Hey, you mind?" he snapped. "He's my brother. Maybe I know some things you don't."

"Maybe."

"Do you think he'd be making this trip if he knew?"

Sarah eyed him coolly. "I think you underestimate him."

"I . . ."

She held up her hand, stopping him. "And don't use that tone of voice with me."

He seemed about to challenge her, then shook his head. "Sorry."

"I know it's rough," she said. "But I think he'll be there for you when it matters."

"I hope so."

Sarah looked out the window and saw David walking toward the van. "Uh-oh." She nudged Marcus. David was carrying a strange knapsack and a leggy blonde was walking beside him.

"What hath God wrought?" Marcus said.

Sarah smiled, shaking her head. "Wasn't she on the road today?"

"I think so."

"I'll bet he offered her a ride."

"You think so?" Marcus said.

"Count on it."

Marcus exhaled loudly. "Well, at least I hope she's the quiet type."

Sarah shook her head. "Not a chance. Look how she's walking."

"Nice legs," Marcus said.

She slapped him playfully in the gut. "I can see that, dummy."

"Then what are you talking about?"

Sarah leaned forward and rested her chin on the steering wheel. "She even *moves* loudly," she said.

Marcus nodded, pulling at his mustache. "I see," he said.

David slid open the side door of the van and put the bag

of food on the seat. "Hi." His smile was full of boyish enthusiasm.

"Hi," Marcus said.

David gestured toward the girl. "Uh, this is Becky Chandler. Becky, this is my brother Marcus, and this is Sarah."

"Hi, Becky," Marcus said.

"Hi," she said nervously.

Sarah smiled. "How's your finger?"

Smiling sheepishly, Becky got up on the seat. "Sorry about that."

"It's okay," Sarah said. "Etiquette of the road."

David began distributing the food. "Becky's gonna ride with us for a while. I offered her a ride."

"Fine." Marcus bit into a French fry.

"Welcome aboard." Sarah set her food on the console.

"Thanks," Becky said.

"We're going to eat on the road," Sarah said. "I want to make the campground before dark."

"You do whatever you want," Becky said. "Even a tornado is not going to stop me from enjoying this burger." She bit into the Quarter Pounder as though she hadn't eaten in a week, then let out several groans of pleasure as she chewed.

Sarah winked at Marcus, fired up the van, and pulled out on Highway 36, heading west.

Becky inhaled her burger in about thirty seconds, then leaned back and rubbed her stomach. "A little health food'll go a long way. I should've ordered a couple more of those."

Marcus looked at her and smiled.

"Hell of the West, huh?" she said. "Sounds great."

"Where are you from, Becky?" Sarah asked.

"The Hell of the *Mid*west—Cleveland." She devoured a couple of fries while the others laughed. "I rode a bike once for ten miles. It was this Battered Wives Bikeathon, and it was real hard. The thrill of victory and the agony of the seat, that's what it was like."

David burst out laughing while Marcus shook his head. This one's a real live wire, Sarah thought. Maybe she was just what they needed after this afternoon's blowup. She sure had put the light back in David's eyes.

Marcus washed down a bite of hamburger and turned around. "How far are you planning to go with us, Becky?"

"Tell you what, Doc." She wiped the corners of her mouth with a napkin. "I'll go pretty far if it feels good."

"All right!" David said, then burst out laughing again.

Sarah looked in the rear view mirror as a catsup-drenched French fry fell from David's hand and landed on Becky's thigh. David looked around for a moment, not knowing what to do, then glanced back at Becky. "Excuse me," he croaked. He picked up the errant fry, shrugged, then wiped the excess catsup from Becky's tanned thigh with his index finger.

"It's okay." A small but noticeable shudder ran down Becky's spine.

David smiled, looking at the fry and his catsupy finger. He glanced at Becky, then at Marcus and Sarah. Finally he shrugged, popped the fry in his mouth and licked the catsup off his finger. "Good to the last drop," he said.

Becky reached out and pinched his arm. Sarah gave Marcus a smile, took a big bite of her burger and began humming a tune to which she didn't even know the title. Young love always made her feel good.

9

Dr. Dennis Conrad strode resolutely through the door of the Jackie Robinson Sports Training Institute, his twelve-year-old son Randolph at his side. Dennis knew that most people would consider his life to be a major success. He had overcome the obstacles of being poor and black, and he had risen to prominence as an athlete and then had made the quantum leap to professional success as a doctor. Not many people who had been dealt his cards could have played so good a hand. Still, there were trade-offs, and Dennis had made his in the sphere of personal relationships. His time had gone into his work, into his becoming somebody, and after six years of marriage and one child, his wife had divorced him because she didn't want to be married to a stranger. Dennis hadn't even tried to fight it. He and his wife had grown too far apart—he didn't think the marriage could be saved if he had all the time in the world.

His main regret was Randolph. Dennis had had enough psychology to know how angry and confused children could get over a divorce. Randolph's revenge on his father took the physical form of body fat—the boy hated athletics, a hatred no doubt encouraged by his mother. Maybe Dennis was wrong, but his strategy in life was always to take the bull by the horns, so when Randolph came down from Milwaukee for his summer month with Dad, Dad put him in a sweatsuit and brought him in for some training.

Randolph took two steps down the corridor and stopped. "I don't like this place."

"You just got here. You're gonna love it."

Randolph shook his head. "It smells bad."

"That's sweat, Randolph." Dennis realized that he actually had a fondness for the odor.

"I know."

"And it doesn't smell bad." He took his son by the arm and started him down the hall again.

"Mama said I didn't have to do this."

"She did, huh?"

"That's right."

Dennis resisted the impulse to say something nasty about his good old used-to-be. "Well, son, your mama isn't here right now."

"She still . . ."

Dennis held up his hand to stop him. "You are in your daddy's sinister clutches now." He nodded for emphasis, smiling diabolically. "And Daddy wants to see his beloved son Randolph sweat his ass off."

"I don't know." Randolph shook his head fearfully.

"Trust me." Dennis patted him on the head. "It's all for your own good." Father and son walked into the activity area.

"Dr. Conrad," a voice said over the intercom. "Telephone, line three."

"Probably Gloria," Dennis muttered, thinking of Randolph's mother.

"What?" Randolph said.

"Nothin'." Dennis gestured to the athletes who were working out on the various machines. "Watch them for awhile. Get yourself some inspiration. I've got to answer the phone."

Randolph wrinkled his lip in disgust.

He's more hardheaded than his mama, Dennis thought. He jerked the phone off the wall and punched a button. "Hello, Dr. Conrad here!" he said fiercely.

"Excuse me," a lady's voice said. "Are you the person who's in charge there?"

He looked around the room for someone to pass the buck to. "I guess you could say I'm in charge." What was this going to be, a malpractice suit? "Who is this?"

"This is Estelle Sommers, Marcus's mother."

"Oh, hello."

"Hello. Do you know Marcus?"

"Sure."

"Well?"

"He's my best friend, ma'am."

"Oh, I'm glad."

"Is everything all right, Mrs. Sommers?" She sounded pretty nervous.

"Well, it's just that I called him at home last night and then again this morning, and there was no answer."

"Right."

"So, uh, being a hysterical sort of person, I was wondering . . ."

"Nothing to worry about, Mrs. Sommers." He hated to lie, but he had no idea how much this woman knew, and he didn't think that enlightening her was his affair.

"Oh, I'm glad." She sounded mighty relieved.

"Marcus and Sarah just went on a little camping trip with David."

"Uh, Sarah?"

"Yeah." Some enlightenment was going to be necessary.

"Who is Sarah?" Mrs. Sommers asked.

"That's the girl Marcus lives with."

"Oh." She paused for a moment. "Well, I just wanted to tell Marcus something. I guess it can wait."

"They'll be back in a week or so. Want me to have him call you if he checks in?"

"That's all right."

"I'll have him call you when he comes back, then."

"Thank you, Dr. Conrad. Thank you for your help."

"My pleasure, ma'am. Nice to meet you."

"Good-bye."

Dennis hung up the phone, took a deep breath, then stared at his son.

Randolph just shook his head as though he didn't want to be a part of any of this.

"You're going to pick a sport and concentrate on it for a month," Dennis said. "And every day you're going to do some calisthenics and some running."

"Oh," Randolph groaned.

"And some sweating."

"Grody," Randolph said.

Dennis glared at him. "Don't tell me they talk that way in Milwaukee, too."

"Milwaukee's a hip city, Dad. Not like this Podunk town."

"Patience, Lord," Dennis pleaded. He clapped his hands together and gave Randolph a very fatherly look. "So, my son. What sport do you want to concentrate on?"

"You mean I have a choice?"

"Sure."

Randolph shrugged. "I like bowling."

"Bowling!" Dennis exploded.

"You said I had a choice."

"Bowling is not a sport!"

"It's . . ."

"It's nothing!" Dennis interrupted. "Bowling is just a big video game."

Randolph shook his head contemptuously. "Hey, don't get all defrosted, huh?"

"What?"

"You heard me," Randolph said. "Don't get all defrosted."

The kid had confidence, he had to give him that. "How the hell does your mother put up with you?"

Randolph spread his palms and shrugged. "Look, Dad. The way I see it is that there aren't any black bowlers, right?"

"I don't know," Dennis said. "I don't follow the game."

"Well, it's true. I mean, there's black basketball players, black football players, we even got one golfer. But bowling, hey, we got zip. Think about it."

Dennis stroked his chin, thinking about it. "Tell you what, kid. I'm gonna take you bowling."

Randolph smiled. "Great, Dad." He started for the door.

Dennis grabbed him by the shoulder. "In a month."

Randolph looked at him as though he'd just been sentenced to the electric chair. "Aw sh . . ."

"Don't say it, son." He pointed to an empty mat, then patted Randolph's soft belly. "I think we'll start with a few sit-ups."

David stood next to Becky in the middle of the camp, looking over the fire at Sarah and Marcus as they set up their sleeping bags. A thin crescent of moon hung in the sky, and the stars were countless and brilliant. He hadn't felt this good in a long time.

Sarah nudged Marcus and pointed to a big tree on the edge of the campsite. "We spent the night in this same place two years ago. Remember?"

Marcus looked at her lovingly. "What do you think?"

She kissed him. "I think you remember."

David couldn't resist. "I think he remembers, Sarah."

"Get out of here," she laughed.

"Okay." He grabbed Becky by the arm. "Come on, let's take a stroll."

"Okay." She followed him down a little hill.

They walked along the edge of a creek in silence for a few moments. David felt so nervous, he couldn't think of anything to say. "How do you like my brother and Sarah?" he blurted out finally.

"Nice," Becky said. "It really looks like they're in love."

David nodded. "They are. Uh, do you have a boyfriend?"

"A few ex-boyfriends," she said. "They're part of the reason I left home for the summer."

"Wouldn't leave you alone, huh?" He imagined that every guy in Cleveland must be after her.

"It wasn't me so much as my parents. I mean, my parents are really nice. Too nice."

"That's nice," David said.

"Funny guy."

"I like to see you smile." He knew he was beginning to sound sappy, but he couldn't help it.

She gave him a big grin. She didn't seem to mind his sappiness. "Anyway, I bring a guy home and my parents fall in love with him."

"And he falls in love with them."

She nodded. "So there were these three guys I'd broken up with, hanging around the house. You know, watching ballgames with my dad, eating my mother's cookies."

"I'd like to meet your folks. They sound wonderful."

"Anyway," she said, "I freaked out. That's what I do when I'm in doubt. I freak out." She tossed a little stone into the creek. "I guess that's how come I ended up eating granola in Kansas."

"Three guys," David said. "You must fall in love easily."

"Oh, it wasn't love." Becky shook her head resolutely. "Not love-love."

"Love-love?" This was getting too metaphysical for him.

"Uh-huh."

"Oh, sure." He nodded as though he understood everything.

She pointed at him. "What's it say on that shirt?"

Involuntarily, he rubbed his hand over the writing on his Institute T-shirt. "It's, uh, Latin."

"That I know," she said. "But what's it say?"

He shrugged off his embarrassment. "It says, 'Once you've got it up, keep it up.'"

"All right!" She clapped her hands and grinned. "Where can I get one?"

In one fluid movement David pulled off the shirt and handed it to her. She gave him a questioning look. "Take it," he said.

"You sure?"

"You bet. A Wisconsin momento, given to you in Kansas by a St. Louis boy."

"Thanks." She took the shirt, obviously pleased. "Uh, why don't we do it like they do it in the Olympics?"

David gave her a questioning look. "How do they do it in the Olympics?"

"You know, exchange T-shirts."

"Fine." The word caught on his throat and barely got out. She began taking off her shirt, and he gasped audibly as he caught sight of her breasts. She gestured for him to turn away, and he complied obediently, gazing across the creek into the night. He cleared his throat, took a deep breath, and suddenly burst into song. "O-o, say can you see, by the dawn's early light."

Becky started laughing. "What're you doing?" she asked.

"If it's the Olympics, you have to play the National Anthem."

"Only if you win."

Her T-shirt landed on his shoulder. "I think I am," he said. He quickly slid into the new shirt. It fit him tighter than a glove. He turned just as her head popped through the top of his shirt. She looked wonderful. I think I'm about to be in love, he thought.

She moved her arms like a conductor. "What so proudly we hail, at the twilight's last gleaming."

David's voice joined hers on the next line. He extended his hand, she took it, and they marched back into camp, singing in a brassy fortissimo, like a pair of true champions. Marcus and Sarah sat up and stared as though they had just seen invaders from another planet.

When Sarah awoke at first light, Marcus was already up. Dressed in his riding gear, he was carefully inspecting his bicycle chain, an incredibly intense expression on his face. Sarah didn't blame him. Tomorrow everything would get very real. The Hell of the West—Marcus's last big race—would begin. The smallest error or equipment malfunction could cost him all the marbles. "Hi." She sat up in her bag and gave him a sleepy smile.

He nodded toward the Coleman stove. "Coffee's on."

"Smells good." She yawned and stretched.

"Hi, Sarah." David spun his front wheel. He didn't look quite as awake as Marcus. She figured he had other things on his mind.

"Star-Spangled David," she said.

He grinned. Becky was still asleep.

Sarah stood up and got herself a cup of coffee, then came back over to Marcus's bike. She rubbed his back. "You feel tense."

"Couldn't imagine why," he said. "It'll pass after a few miles."

"What's on for today?"

"Little bit of everything. Make sure Junior there is ready for the big time."

"Bring it on," David said. "I'll ride to the top of Pike's Peak backwards."

"Hey," Marcus said. "Nothing like a little confidence to start the day."

Becky rolled over, groaned, sat up and shook the sleep out of her head.

"Morning." David's smile was as wide as the sky.

She nodded at him. "Leaving already?"

David pointed to Marcus. "He's a slave driver, what can I tell you?"

"Get yourself some coffee," Sarah said. "I'll whip us up some breakfast. You'd probably like some granola."

The others laughed as Becky's face fell.

"How about some bacon and eggs?" Sarah said.

"That's the best thing I've heard all day," Becky said.

David reached out and pulled her to her feet. "The day is young," he said.

"The day is getting old," Marcus said. "Let's get out there and bust a sweat."

"Okay, Pops." David buckled on his toestraps. "Lead me to it."

"See you all later." Marcus mounted up and headed out of camp.

"We'll catch up to you," Sarah yelled.

"Not if you don't step on the gas." David followed his brother, then turned back to the girls. "Bye, Becky."

"Bye. Watch it!" she yelled, just saving him from running into a tree.

Sarah laughed, watching the brothers disappear over a small rise.

"David sure seems happy this morning," Becky said.

Sarah patted her on the back. "I couldn't imagine why."

"You mean he's not always this way?"

"Not really."

"Oh."

Sarah went over to the cooler and pulled out a pound of bacon. "You may not know it, Becky, but I think you've saved the Sommers brothers racing team."

Becky gave her a "Who, me?" look, then smiled. "I'm always happy to help."

They ate breakfast and cleaned up the campsite, then loaded everything in the van and took off. Whatever trepidation Sarah had felt about Becky was gone, and she was looking forward to having her around during the tense days of the race. Becky was a little spacy, but so were most nineteen-year-olds who were just waking up to the fact that there was more to life than what their parents had told them. Becky was enthusiastic and essentially good-hearted, not some lazy, depressed flake. Sarah knew she could count on her to pull her weight if it became necessary. Mainly, Becky was just fun to be around.

"They ride, you drive, is that the deal?" Becky asked once they were rolling down the highway.

"Not all the time," Sarah said. "But a lot of the day is like that."

"Guess you don't break too many speed laws, huh?"

"Not too many."

"Must be lonely, though."

Sarah shrugged. "Not really. Gives me time to think. Plus, I get to see a lot of the country."

"You seem kind of peaceful inside," Becky said. "Guess it doesn't bother you to be alone."

"Sometimes it's nice."

"Oh, there they are!" Becky pointed ahead to the bicycling brothers.

"That's one thing nice about the van," Sarah said. "You can always catch up." She pulled within a hundred feet, watching David and Marcus carefully. After a few moments, she nodded approval. They both seemed loose, and full of energy. Quick, clean reactions to each other's moves. She allowed herself to think that maybe they could win the race.

Marcus began to zigzag all over the road, David following him as though he were his shadow.

Becky was moving her head back and forth like a fan at a tennis match. "What's going on?" she asked after a moment.

"Shake and break," Sarah said.

Becky gave her a questioning look.

"It's a race tactic. If you're trying to make a solo breakway and you've got a wheelsucker hanging on to you, you shake and break to shake him off."

"What's a wheelsucker?" Becky asked.

Sarah laughed, thinking how stupid the word must sound to someone who didn't know. "That's somebody who drafts all the time and won't take his turn up front. It's a lot easier to ride if someone else is taking the wind resistance for you."

Becky nodded. "Boy, you learn something every day." She pointed to David. "Pull up a little bit."

Sarah got closer to the brothers. Becky leaned out the window and yelled at David, "Come on, you wheelsucker!"

He flashed her a look of surprise, then smiled.

Becky shook her fist at him. "Get up there!"

David followed Marcus through another couple of moves, then suddenly turned to the outside and shot past him. Marcus gave him a split-second glance of surprise, then took off after him. Good reaction, Sarah thought. There had been virtually no loss of concentration.

"Look at that," Becky said.

"Here we go." Sarah accelerated a little as the brothers flew down the highway in front of the van. Marcus was now on David's wheel, but it only took a few seconds before David began trying to shake him off. David had learned his lessons well. She just hoped the pressure of the actual race wouldn't throw off his concentration. She slowed down a little, letting them get ahead. As they began climbing a small hill, Marcus pulled out, and the brothers raced side by side to the top. "Damn, they look good!" Sarah said as they disappeared over the crest.

"They sure do."

Suddenly there was an explosion, and the van began to bounce.

Becky gave Sarah a panicked look.

"Shit!" Sarah said, braking and pulling off the road. "I knew that left rear tire wasn't long for this world."

"Guess we'll never catch 'em now," Becky said.

"Ever change a tire before?"

Becky shook her head. "But I think I'm about to learn."

10

David thought he had already used up most of his power, but as he stood up and sprinted for the top of the hill, the energy just kept coming and coming. He was aware of Marcus's heavy breathing beside him, but David refused to look at him, focusing instead on the top of the hill and the imaginary finish line he had put there. Whether or not he beat his brother across the line he would never know. He looked over the moment after they crested the hill, and it would have taken some micromeasuring device to tell whose front wheel was out in front. But David knew immediately that that wasn't what mattered. The brothers looked at each other and smiled wearily. They had both just run one hell of a race, and Marcus's look seemed to be telling him that if they could do it that well in the Hell of the West, they would probably go home winners.

"Not bad," Marcus said after they had coasted for a couple of minutes.

David took a deep breath. "Nice little warm-up."

"Warm-up?" Marcus actually sounded worried that David was going to try to pull something.

"Sure." David pointed off to their right front where a large herd of cattle was grazing. Five cowboys were trotting along on horses beside the herd.

"I see 'em," Marcus said.

"Think we can beat 'em?"

Marcus looked at him for a moment. "You gotta be nuts, you know that?"

"I do know that, Big Brother," David said. "You think I'd be out here in the first place if I wasn't nuts?" He cut loose with another of his patented coyote howls, then, as the cowboys looked at him, he did a wheelie for about a hundred feet. When his front wheel hit the pavement, he began to sprint.

"Son of a bitch!" Marcus bellowed.

David guffawed, waving to the cowboys. Instantly, they accepted his challenge, letting loose with rebel yells as they spurred their horses into gallops. David looked over his shoulder. Marcus hadn't taken long deciding to race—he was already bearing down on David. The younger brother faced forward and began pedaling like a madman. He was feeling so good that he thought he might explode.

The wind whistled past his ears, and his own breath came forth in great gasps. He heard the pounding of horses' hooves, and looked over his right shoulder to see the cowboys gaining on them. He looked back further, hoping to see the van on the highway, but it was nowhere in sight. They must have stopped for something. Too bad. He wished Becky could see him now.

"She ain't gonna help you now, bro." Marcus blew by him on the left.

David bore down on him, pulling to within inches of his rear wheel, then easing up as the wind resistance lessened. They rode that way for a couple of minutes, the distance between them remaining the same, almost as if they were parts of a statue in perpetual motion.

Without thinking about it, he knew that Marcus was tiring, and instinctively he pulled out and took the lead, allowing his brother to draft off him for a while. In truth, he felt so strong that he thought he could ride like this forever. The cowboys thundering down on them were a beautiful sight, like the James Gang riding herd on a train in a movie he'd seen. Still, the brothers kept ahead of them, chasing the horizon. Tomorrow it would all be for real, David thought, wondering if any moment could ever be as real as the one he was in right now. The crystal blue sky was dotted with small cumulus puffs which he thought of as smoke signals testifying to some glorious fact of life. The thought of his own death did nothing to dampen his spirits. He could live another hundred years and not experience life as intensely as he was experiencing it now. He howled with affirmation once again, and, delirious with joy, pumped harder and harder until he and his brother left the galloping cowboys behind.

Sarah nodded with approval as Becky tightened the last lug nut on the new wheel and stood up. "Very good."

"Thanks."

"Thank you." Sarah took the lug wrench and threw it on top of the flat tire in the back of the van. "We'll get that tire fixed tonight." She gave the jack a kick and the new tire hit the ground.

"You sure know how to do a lot of stuff," Becky said.

"Now you can do it too."

"Not just tires. I mean, you seem to know a lot about a lot of things."

Sarah shrugged. She felt a little embarrassed.

"I guess you and Marcus are kind of a team, huh?"

"In a lot of ways."

"Uh, are you in love with him?"

Sarah smiled. "Yes, I am."

Becky seemed tickled by the news. "Love-love?" she asked.

Sarah looked at her for a moment. This was one she hadn't heard. "What's love-love?"

"It's, uh, you know. It's when . . ."

Sarah held up her hand to stop her, staring at the dirty van with the bicycles on top that was bearing down on them. "Hold it." Her stomach went a little hollow and her heartbeat picked up. Muzzin. She knew she'd be seeing him sooner or later. She preferred later.

The van slowed, then its brakes screeched as it fish-tailed onto the shoulder, stopping perpendicular to the road.

"Don't worry," Sarah said to a surprised Becky, then she picked up the jack and tossed it into the back of the van. "I know 'em."

She was actually glad to see Jerome, the easygoing black man who was Muzzin's partner. He smiled warmly at her. "Hello, Sarah."

"Hi, Jerome."

He shrugged, a hint of an apology for Muzzin's stopping. "It's been a long time."

"It has."

Muzzin stood beside him, a good six inches taller, a malicious look on his face. The same malicious look she had come to hate. His other partners, two young blond racers, stayed in the van. Muzzin finally smiled at her. "I said to Jerome, Jerome, I said, that sure looks like Marcus's van. Our old team van." He paused a minute to let it sink in. "Hello, Geronimo."

"Hello, Muzzin." She kept it cool. No emotion either way. But she knew he was going to start digging right away.

"Where is he?" Muzzin said.

She pointed down the road. "Riding."

Muzzin nodded, a cynical smile on his face. "He's great when it comes to training."

Jerome tugged his arm. "Come on, Muzzin. What do you say? Don't start in."

Muzzin pulled his arm away, then looked at his partner. "You know, Jerome, women are a real mystery. In racing, the best man always wins. What the hell is it about some women that makes them fall for quitters like Marcus Sommers?"

Jerome looked away.

Sarah glanced at Becky who was staring intently at Muzzin, taking it all in. "Even a bigger mystery, Jerome," Sarah said, "is what made *some* women ever fall in love with a rabid dog like Muzzin." She stared coldly at her ex-husband. He was still tall and handsome, but whatever joy he'd possessed had been extinguished by his ferocious monomania to win, win, win. The winning was important to Marcus, too, but there was a whole different quality to his desire.

"Hey, come on, you two," Jerome said.

Muzzin paid his partner no mind. "You tell Marcus, Sarah."

"Tell him what?" she snapped.

"You don't have to tell him I'm going to win, because he already knows that."

"Sure," she said.

Muzzin's face hardened. "But you tell him I'm going to make him bleed before I beat him."

She blinked, biting the inside of her lip in an attempt to show no emotion. "I don't deliver messages, Muzzin. Sometimes I don't even hear them."

"He'll quit," Muzzin snorted. He pointed to his own chest with his thumb. "I'll see to that." His eyes narrowed. "I'll make him die in those mountains."

Sarah jerked backward as though someone had slapped her. Then, very slowly, she bent down and picked up a jagged rock that felt like it weighed ten pounds. "Jerome," she said, "I think of you as a friend."

He eyed the rock, nodding vigorously.

"So, do me a favor," she said.

"Anything."

"Take that goddamn cannibal out of my face before I kill him."

Jerome pulled Muzzin's arm, more strongly than before. "Hey, I'm Jerome."

Muzzin looked at him.

"And you're The Cannibal," Jerome said. He pointed to Sarah. "And that's a big rock. Come on."

Muzzin didn't move. Sarah slid her foot forward slightly, hoping he'd feel threatened, hoping he might remember a couple of the fights they'd had. He didn't call her Geronimo for no reason.

After a moment he gave a contemptuous snort and let Jerome escort him back to the van.

Sarah took a quick look at Becky. The girl was looking at Sarah, her mouth wide open in amazement. Sarah turned away and watched Muzzin open the door to his van.

One of the blond racers stuck his head out and pointed at Marcus's van. "That belongs to the guy who always gets second place, huh?"

Sarah almost chucked the rock at him.

"Shutup, Goldilocks," Muzzin said. "Let's see you get second place before you make fun of it." He climbed in and slammed the door.

Sarah smiled and shook her head. Muzzin still had a

fragment of his code left. Never mock anyone you couldn't beat. He was a hell of a racer, she had to admit that.

Sarah watched Muzzin's van until it crested the hill and dipped out of sight, then she turned and heaved the rock into the weeds at the side of the road.

Becky eyed her, nodding her head with approval. "Well, I'll be a Fig Newton!" she said. "I'm standing here next to a woman with a past."

Sarah shrugged. "One ex-husband," she said. "Not much of a past."

"Looks like a hell of a past to me," Becky said. "You were married to that guy?"

"Um hm."

"And you survived?"

"I'm here, aren't I?"

Becky nodded. "And you must be one tough lady."

Maybe so, Sarah thought. Maybe so. She nodded toward the van. "Let's go find the boys."

Becky's eyes brightened. "Sounds good to me," she said. "But first I want to get something." She rummaged around in the weeds until she found Sarah's rock. "Eureka!" she said, holding it aloft.

Sarah shook her head. "What do you want with that?"

"Souvenir," Becky said. "My first memento from the Hell of the West."

"You're something else, you know that?"

"So they say." Becky tossed the rock into the air and caught it. "But so are you."

"Let's go," Sarah said.

Marcus pulled even with David, and together they flew down the highway, finally passing an intersection of fence where the cowboys were forced to stop and turn north. The bicyclists and the horsemen waved to each other, then the brothers faced west and ceased their frantic pumping. At once exhausted and exhilarated, Marcus turned and smiled at David. His little brother grinned back at him, nodding his head. Marcus held his fist aloft and shook it, feeling as though he had just won an important victory. It was the look in David's eyes that made him feel so good. He wasn't sure what to call it. "Killer instinct" sounded too rough; maybe "the right stuff" was better. Regardless of what it was called, Marcus knew in his bones that David had what it took to be a champion, to put together all the different elements required to be a winner. Marcus reached over and patted him on the back. "Not bad, big guy. Not bad at all."

David took a deep breath, obviously touched by his brother's approval. "Think so?"

Marcus nodded. "I know so."

"Were we going as fast as I think we were?"

"Uh huh."

"Boy." David spat onto the shoulder of the road, then took a drink from his water bottle.

"And we're going to go that fast tomorrow."

David touched the water bottle to his head in mock salute. "Yes, sir."

They pedaled silently down the highway for a few more miles, Marcus feeling his heartbeat drop quickly back into the normal zone as his burning legs began to cool. Finally he said, "Let's take it back."

"Already?"

Marcus nodded. "I think that'll do it for today."

"If you say so, Coach."

They turned and headed east, the sun now high overhead. "No sense using up all our energy today," Marcus said. "Save a little for tomorrow. All our moves are solid, and I just don't think there's anything more we can do to get ready."

"Sounds good to me," David said.

"We'll check the bikes over after lunch, then maybe ride 'em a few miles this afternoon."

"We showed those cowboys, didn't we?" David said.

"Yeah."

"The Sommers bicycle cavalry." David laughed. "I wonder how John Wayne would've liked that race."

"He would've beat us," Marcus said.

They both burst out laughing, Marcus leaning back in his seat and letting go with a prolonged shriek. It felt great to get rid of the tension, to feel so loose—and confident—this close to the beginning of the race. Then he saw the van. He suddenly stopped laughing. He knew David was looking at him, but he couldn't take his eyes off the approaching vehicle with the four bicycles on top glistening in the sunlight.

"Marcus?"

He glanced quickly at his brother. "It's Muzzin." Again he stared ahead, meeting Muzzin's cold, hateful gaze as the van roared past them. Jerome gave a little wave, but Marcus couldn't bring himself to return the gesture. He turned and watched the van for a few seconds, then faced front again.

"Looks like a real sweetheart," David said.

"Whatever he is," Marcus said, "don't forget that he's a tremendous racer." He could feel the tension starting again. He knew he was going to have a real race on his hands tomorrow. "Don't get too close to him." It was almost as if he was talking to himself, reminding himself. "And don't listen to anything he has to say. He knows every sucker move in the book, and he's probably invented a few new ones since the last time he raced."

"I'll watch out for him."

"You just ride your own race. Once you start reacting to him, you're finished."

"Got the picture, Boss." David tried to sound nonchalant, but Marcus could hear the beginnings of fear in his voice.

"Anyway," Marcus said. "Maybe he'll get a flat tire."

"If the gods are on our side," David said.

Marcus pointed to the approaching van. "At least the goddesses are on our side."

Sarah pulled onto the shoulder and stopped, and the brothers swung around to the rear of the van and wearily undid their toestraps. Sarah came back and Marcus gave her a knowing grin. "You see him?" he asked.

She nodded. "You too?"

"Yeah."

"He say anything?"

"Not a word," Marcus said. "But if looks could kill . . ."

"We'd've been splattered all over the pavement," David said.

"Did you talk to him?" Marcus asked.

She shrugged casually. "We had a few words."

"A few words?!" Becky appeared at her side, a large rock in her hand. "You call that a few words?"

"What happened?" Marcus asked.

"His usual pleasant conversation," Sarah said. "Nothing out of the ordinary."

"Whoo!" Becky rolled her eyes heavenward. "If that's ordinary, I'd hate to see that guy when he's mad. I mean, you got one fine woman here, Marcus."

He smiled at Sarah. "What?"

Before she could say anything, Becky said, "Well, first he gets goin' about how he's going to ride you to death out in the mountains, then Sarah picks up this rock here and says to his buddy Jerome, 'Take that goddamn cannibal out of my sight before I kill him.' Wow!" Becky looked reverently at Sarah. "Then Jerome goes, 'Hey, I'm Jerome. You're the goddamn cannibal and that's a big rock.'" Becky held out the rock for them all to look at. "Oh, man, you missed it all. Sarah was so tough. So *cool*. I'm keeping this rock, believe me. I'll be taking it back to college."

Marcus put his arm around Sarah and gave her a warm smile. "My tough little lady."

"He was horrible," she said.

"Sounds like he was going for the jugular."

"It's the only place he knows."

"Well," Marcus said, "he's not getting near mine. Now let's rack these bikes and get back on the road, then I'll buy you all some lunch."

They drove for half an hour so he and David could cool off, then stopped at a small café and consumed a gargantuan lunch. Plenty of energy for tomorrow. The Gerard team was also eating there, and joking with them helped take Marcus's mind off Muzzin and the dark cloud he'd planted there. Marcus had to give him credit—the guy could psych-out the most tough-minded person alive. Well, Marcus was going to do his best not to fall for it. As they drove west through the late afternoon and early evening, they passed (and were passed by) more and more vans of racers. The waves, shouts, smiles, and honking horns made Marcus feel a kinship with his fellow racers that Muzzin had made him forget. Muzzin was alone, outside of all of this, sharing no feelings of camaraderie with the other riders. If they all died tomorrow, he'd be perfectly happy. When Marcus thought back on his career as a racer, he remembered lots of things: the hard training, victories, losses, silly mistakes, brilliant strategies. But what stood out was the human contact; he had made a lot of good friends and met many outstanding people. He wouldn't trade that in for all the trophies in the world.

As the sun dipped below the towering peaks of the Rocky Mountains, Marcus stopped the van, then he and David got out and made the last mechanical adjustments on their bikes. They strapped in and cranked out a quick five miles, and when Marcus was certain that everything was perfect, they stopped and fastened the bikes back in the racks.

He climbed back in the van, taking the driver's seat again.

"All set?" Sarah asked.

"Nothin' more to do," he said. He gave her a little kiss and got back on the road.

"All we gotta do now is win the race," David said from the back.

"Beat The Cannibal," Becky said. "That's my slogan from here on out."

Marcus and Sarah smiled at each other. Beat The Cannibal indeed! he thought.

11

"Ladies and gentlemen," boomed the impersonal voice over the public address system. "Welcome to the first circuit of the Hell of the West bicycle race." David's stomach suddenly felt a little more hollow as he realized that the start of the race was only a couple of minutes away. He looked up at the fluttering banner above the starting line. "HELL OF THE WEST," it said, almost like a challenge hurled in his face. The PA continued: "Today's race takes place on the dreaded Morgul Bismarck. It's a world championship-quality course, which offers little shade, steep hills, fast descents and a gut-wrenching climb to the finish line that sits atop the devastating wall. This is a race of seven laps totalling ninety-one miles, a grueling test for any rider unused to riding in a pack."

"But other than that, it's a piece of cake," David said to Becky, who was standing beside him.

"I'm glad I'll be sitting this one out." She looked around at all the brightly colored jerseys.

"There are ninety-six riders in the field," the announcer said. "Only the top forty-eight get to ride stages two and three after today."

"There's more buns here than at the Wonder bakery," Becky said.

"That's one way of looking at it." Marcus gave David a nervous smile. He was trying to appear casual, but David knew his mind was focused totally on the race.

"Here come some more vehicles," the announcer said. "Let's keep the roadway clear so they can get through, please. We have team cars from Mexico, Great Britain, Italy, Norway, New Zealand and Holland."

Sarah took Becky by the arm. "Let's go get in the van." She gave Marcus a little kiss. "Do well."

He nodded, staring straight ahead.

"You too." Becky gave David a playful squeeze.

"Okay," he croaked. His throat was dry and he was nervous as hell. He watched the girls walk away, glad to see Becky wearing his cowboy hat. Actually, he felt a little naked without it. Maybe he should have worn the thing for such an important event, like Slim Pickens when he rode the H-bomb in *Dr. Strangelove*. Then he looked at the terrain and decided it was better to be wearing a crash helmet.

"All set?" Marcus reached over and patted him on the back.

"Bring it on," David said, fighting a surge of feelings of inadequacy. He'd never raced in a pack before; he hadn't trained on *really* steep hills.

The PA system crackled again. "With us here today, wearing the stars-and-stripes jersey—and it's a good thing he's not in the bike race—is, ladies and gentlemen, Eddie Mercyx. He's with us right here under the banner."

David listened to the applause of the spectators and wriggled his right foot in the toestrap to make sure it was secure.

"All drivers, you should be in your vehicles."

He looked over as Becky and Sarah waved from the van. He barely managed a smile in return.

"Ladies and gentlemen, we are minutes from the start. We would like to introduce you to some of the riders who are going to be participating in today's event, beginning with the U.S. National Team."

As the announcer rattled off the names, David looked down at his own blue jersey, donated by ShaverSport, a relatively obscure sporting goods manufacturer that Marcus had found to sponsor them when he no longer wished to be part of another team. David knew absolutely no one in the race besides his brother. And no one knew him. The anonymity was weird—just like on his imaginary races through the Missouri and Illinois countryside.

"Ladies and gentlemen, the Soviet national team, led by the defending Olympic champion, Sergei Belov."

Five riders in red inched up to the starting line. Belov was huge, and David thought he carried too much weight to be a very fast racer. But he also looked incredibly powerful, and he probably had the stamina of an ox. David looked at Marcus who seemed to be studying each racer, going over his mental notes on what he would have to do to beat each one.

"And finally, ladies and gentlemen, the green-shirted Seven-Eleven team, led by our own 1980 Olympic Trial winner, two-time National Champion, and the winner of last year's Hell of the West, Barry 'The Cannibal' Muzzin."

The crowd cheered with twice the enthusiasm they had shown for the Russians, and Muzzin did absolutely nothing to acknowledge it. Jerome tried to raise his arm, but Muzzin shook him off. Belov offered a gentlemanly handshake.

Muzzin reached into the back pocket of his jersey and pulled out a banana. "Stick that, Belov." He put it in the Russian's outstretched hand.

Belov regarded the banana for a moment, then narrowed his eyes angrily and dropped it to the ground. He faced forward as Muzzin gave him a nasty little smile.

"Ladies and gentlemen, our honorary starter for the Hell of the West, stage number one. The greatest racing cyclist in the history of the sport, Mr. Eddie Mercyx." The crowd applauded politely, then quieted for the start of the race. "We will be started on the sound of the pistol."

David shook his head vigorously and took a couple of deep breaths.

"Riders ready!"

He looked straight ahead. Nothing to do but go that way.

"Timers ready!"

He rubbed his hands together, then gripped the handlebars. Only ninety-one miles, he thought. Less than he rode every day.

The gun sounded and a roar went up from the crowd. David began to move with the sea of riders around him. He adjusted his left toestrap, noticing his front wheel squishing over the banana that Belov had dropped on the road.

"We are underway!" the announcer yelled. "The Hell of the West, stage number one. Let's hear it for a big send-off. The Hell of the West, stage one. Underway!"

For a moment David heard the send-off, then the sound was lost amidst the grunts and groans of the racers as they shifted gears and pulled away from the starting line. David's mind seemed to go blank as the bikes plunged down a steep descent, Muzzin in the lead. Follow Marcus, David told himself, pumping hard to stay right behind his brother. Other riders grazed him as either he or they weaved as he moved up through the pack. He thought they had actually passed a few of the others.

They hit the bottom of the hill and started to climb, David still too nervous and dazzled to focus on much more than speeding forward.

"Hey, watch it!" someone in a blue-and-gray jersey said as David weaved a bit to the side and brushed him.

"Sorry," David gasped. He shouldn't have said it. Don't waste the breath, he thought. Christ, this hill was steep. Still, they managed to climb a little closer to the head of the pack. Muzzin crested the hill first with Jerome and their two blond partners. Then came the Russians, led by Belov, then the Japanese Sunnino team, then the Gita team from Italy.

The course leveled out briefly, and the fierce jockeying for position eased off. David tried not to let the slackened pace lull him. He stayed right behind Marcus, less confused and more alert now, waiting for something to happen. He would follow Marcus as long as it was possible. He knew that he would be on his own sooner than he wanted to be.

The Gita team began to move, and Marcus signaled to David. They swung out and blasted by the Sunnino team. It seemed easy, David thought, standing up and pumping. They pulled within a few feet of the Gita team, then Marcus slowed down, seemingly content to follow the Italians and draft off them for a while.

They started into another climb, Marcus studying the head of the pack. Muzzin took a drink of water, then put his bottle back in the cage. His hand reached for his gearshift.

"Here we go, David," Marcus muttered.

Muzzin turned to his teammates. "Enough of this Sunday stroll," he said. "Let's hurt a little." Suddenly he stood up and began to sprint.

"Let's go!" Marcus bellowed, standing up.

David didn't miss a beat, taking off like a bat out of hell. He shot past Marcus who immediately jumped on his wheel, then the two of them blasted by the Gita team who had yet to finish reacting to Muzzin.

David felt terrific, and a sudden burst of energy kept him standing up and sprinting right to the top of the hill, where he and Marcus caught the Russians. There he was, David Sommers, shoulder to shoulder with Sergei Belov. For a split second he was tempted to let go with a coyote howl, then they crested the hill and he nearly howled with anguish instead. Suddenly he was looking down the steepest drop he had ever seen. He looked around, not knowing quite what to do. Already he was going too fast. He shifted, touched his brakes and wobbled a bit. Someone passed him. Another cursed him. He heard grunts in different languages as a few more bikes raced past him. "Hold the line, goddammit!" someone howled. He tried to catch Marcus, but someone cut in front of him. He hit the brake again. The people lining the road went by in a blur, yelling, cheering, clapping, exhorting. What the hell was he doing? For a moment he feared choking the whole thing, tearing through the crowd and plunging off the mountain, dying even sooner than he expected to anyway. He touched the brake again and again someone yelled at him. "Shit!" he mumbled. They should have spent more time practicing on some of these hills. Somehow he made it through the turn, but when he looked up the next hill he saw at least twenty-five bikes ahead of him. He and Marcus were hopelessly separated. Any strategy that depended on their racing together was useless. He cursed himself, then admonished himself to get it together and continue racing. They were only on the first lap. He still had plenty of time to go.

Legs on fire, Marcus stood up and sprinted to the top of the wall, his eyes moving from Belov's heaving buttocks to the digital lap meter as it blinked from 5 to 4. Belov and two of the Russians were a few meters ahead of him, Muzzin and one of his blond jackrabbits five meters ahead of them.

"Ladies and gentlemen," the PA boomed, "three laps down and four to go. Four to go. Four laps to go."

Got the message, Marcus thought, sitting down. Not even halfway. *Almost* halfway. No negative thoughts.

"Barry Muzzin is leading the group, ladies and gentlemen, followed by his Seven-Eleven teammate, Jim McCrary. Then come Sergei Belov and Yuri Golyadkin of the Russian team, then Marcus Sommers of ShaverSport. Each lap yet to come on this grueling course will take its toll on the riders. Only the toughest will be among the first forty-eight who will go on to contest stages two and three of the Hell of the West."

Tell me about it, Marcus thought, looking back over his shoulder. He saw Jerome and the other blonde, the other Russians, the Japanese, Italians, and French. But no David. Damn! he thought, facing forward and racing down the descent.

Muzzin looked back and coldly regarded the group behind him, then faced front again. Belov glanced over his shoulder, looking as if he were trying to solve some problem in physics. I'm still here, Muzzin, Marcus thought, content to lay back a few meters and not challenge the leader until everything was on the line. He was feeling good and racing well, and he knew he could stay with Muzzin no matter what he tried.

Halfway up the next hill, he looked back again, and again there was no David. He hoped everything was all right. He knew that David had the speed and endurance to stay with the leading pack; he also knew that David's inexperience as a racer would work against him, at least for two or three laps. But the kid was a fast learner and had great reactions. Marcus expected he would be catching up by the sixth or seventh lap. Anyway, David was on his own now, and there wasn't anything Marcus could do but ride the best race possible. The main thing was to beat Muzzin, and the way things were going, he thought he could do it. He wasn't too worried about Belov, but he was smart enough not to count him out. You never counted out anyone in a race like this, unless the person had some fatal flaw that consistently ruined his races. Even the unknowns could surprise you—Marcus's very hope with David.

He stood up and sprinted to the top of the next hill, drafting a little off Golyadkin. At the crest he looked over his shoulder and saw the van coming up on him, then he faced forward and flew down the curving descent. It was a bitch, but he felt terrific, holding the line as the wind whipped past, the clothing of the spectators making a kaleidoscopic blur to his left. He could see how David probably lost some time here. The hill was scary, no doubt about it.

Marcus negotiated the descent perfectly, the breakaway group bunching even closer so that no more than five meters separated the first five riders. McCrary jumped in front of Muzzin, and Golyadkin put Belov in his draft. Marcus felt so good that for a moment he was tempted to go for the lead, but he decided to keep hanging back. There was still plenty of time.

"Shit!" he whispered when he heard the air escaping from his rear tire. No time for regrets, he thought quickly, raising his hands and drifting to the right. It pained him to see the group move away from him. I'll be back, boys, he thought, looking over his shoulder to make sure the van was there.

"Pull over!" Sarah said suddenly.

"Huh?" Becky was crusing slowly in the van.

"Quick!"

"What's wrong?" Now she noticed Marcus, his arms up, moving to the side of the road.

"He's got a flat!" Sarah reached over the seat and grabbed a spare tire. "Pull right up behind him!"

"Yes, ma'am." Becky was suddenly alert, realizing how important this could be. She'd been to the Indianapolis 500 once, and had been amazed at how fast the pit crews could change tires. She could see how important the time was here.

Sarah opened the door and hopped out of the van before it had stopped completely. Marcus had his feet out of the toestraps, and was just standing there, staring straight ahead as the other racers pulled away from him. "One, one thousand," Becky muttered, deciding to time Sarah. She didn't even get to ten before Sarah yelled "Go!" and tightened the clamp on the rear wheel as Marcus pulled back on the highway. Sarah walked nonchalantly back to the van, carrying the flat.

"I'm impressed," Becky said.

"I'm *de*pressed," Sarah replied. "He didn't need that."

"You changed that tire in less than ten seconds."

Sarah climbed in the van and put the tire in the back. "I've done it in seven."

Becky pulled back on the road. "You guys must practice a lot."

"Stuff's crucial." Sarah was dead serious.

"You tell him about David?"

"I told him he was back there. Maybe we ought to swing around again, see what place he's in."

Becky accelerated. "You think Marcus'll catch up?"

"I hope so." Sarah shook her head and stared out the window. "They're going awfully fast. And he's got a lot more than the ten seconds to make up. You know, slowing down, getting going again, it all adds up."

"Maybe one of the others'll have a flat."

"Could happen. Nothing to count on, though."

"Just yourself, huh?" Becky and Sarah waved as they rode by Marcus. He kept his eyes straight ahead. He looked like he was really working.

"That's it," Sarah said.

"Sounds just like life," Becky said. She sure was around a lot of self-reliant people.

Two packs of riders had whizzed by Marcus during the tire-changing operation, but he passed one group right after they had started the fifth lap and moved by the other group on the curving descent of the sixth lap. Muzzin and Belov were maybe one hundred meters ahead of him, and Marcus had to fight himself from trying to make up the distance too fast. He had to pace himself now, always closing the distance, but not using up so much energy that he'd fold when the pressure was really on. It had become a thinking man's race. Marcus knew he could win; he also knew that he could lose if he didn't play it right.

He raced hard, he rested, drafting when he could, taking the wind himself when it was necessary. Whenever Muzzin slowed down Marcus would push for a few extra seconds, then rest himself, the gap having been closed by a few more meters. He knew when Muzzin was going to sprint, so he would start his own sprint a few seconds before, narrowing the distance inch by inch.

As they hit the ascent to the wall at the conclusion of the sixth lap, Marcus was only twenty-five meters back. He wanted to chase Muzzin to the top, beat him on the sixth lap and really give him something to think about for the rest of the race. Psych-out the psycher-outer. But Marcus held back, barely managing to maintain the distance as Muzzin—perhaps sensing his intentions—made a ferocious sprint to the top.

"Ladies and gentlemen, one lap to go!" the announcer yelled. "One lap to go, comin' up on one to go. One lap to go!"

Shut up, Marcus thought. Up ahead a photographer stepped out to get a picture of Muzzin. The Cannibal rode right at him, and probably would have knocked him down had not the hapless photog scrambled back into the crowd. Muzzin waved the finger at him. You just lost two more seconds, Marcus thought. Muzzin's loathing of the press occasionally interfered with his rationality.

Marcus saw Sarah up ahead and quickly took his empty water bottle out of the cage. He tossed it to the ground beside her, grabbing the full one from her along with half a sandwich. He hated to waste the time eating, but he knew he needed the nourishment. He vacuumed the sandwich in three quick bites, nodding gratefully at Sarah as she said, "You can get him, Marcus. You can get him on this lap." Amen, he thought, starting down the descent that began the final lap. He took a quick drink of water, sprayed some on his neck, then put the bottle in the cage. "Okay, Cannibal," he muttered. "I'm gonna eat you up."

Sarah picked the plastic water bottle off the pavement and walked back to where Becky was standing with the provisions for David. One more lap, she thought. She nodded to herself with guarded confidence. Marcus hadn't looked as tired as she thought he'd be. With Muzzin, you never knew. He could be ready to drop dead and his face would still be full of his inexhaustible fury.

"He's doin' real well," Becky said.

"Looks that way, doesn't it?"

Becky grinned enthusiastically. "Think he'll win?"

"Sure."

"Me too." Becky looked back for David. "Are you and Marcus planning to get married?" she asked casually.

"No." That was the fact, and Sarah said it plainly.

"Never?" Becky asked.

Sarah shook her head. "Never."

Becky looked at her for a moment. "Don't you want to?"

"Oh yes," Sarah said. "I do."

"I see."

I doubt it, Sarah thought. Generally, she didn't like questions about her personal life, but Becky's didn't bother her that much. They were innocent enough, after all. Becky was genuinely curious, not some person who was prying for the sake of gossip. Time would teach her that everybody didn't take so kindly to such questions.

Becky smiled at her. "So Marcus doesn't want to get married, huh?"

Sarah didn't know how she was going to get out of this one, then it was the race that saved her. She pointed over Becky's shoulder to where David was laboring up to the feed zone.

"Uh-oh," Becky said, suddenly forgetting her interest in Sarah and Marcus's love life. "Have I got everything?"

"You're fine," Sarah said. "Just make sure he gets ahold of it." Sarah turned and looked at the counter that was recording the positions of the racers who finished the laps. Forty-five, forty-six, forty-seven, forty-eight, forty-nine. She turned back to the road and three more bikes went by her before David's. He looked more confused than tired. "Fifty-three, David!" she yelled. "You've got to move up!"

"Move up, David!" Becky echoed, handing him the water bottle and sandwich. "I know you can do it."

He flashed her a weary smile, then stuffed the sandwich in his mouth.

Two more racers blasted by, refusing food and passing David as he took a drink of water.

"Oh no!" Becky said.

"Don't worry," Sarah said. "They'll crap out from lack of nourishment."

"You sure? It's only thirteen miles."

"I'm sure." Sarah smiled. "It's a *long* thirteen miles."

By the time they reached the bottom of the murderous, curving descent, Marcus had closed the gap to less than ten meters—perfect striking distance. On the next grade he stood up and sprinted, passing a surprised Belov and pulling up even with Muzzin. The Cannibal gave him a cold look, then let out a blood-curdling yell and sprinted on ahead. Marcus let him go, but kept the distance at five meters. The main thing was that he had planted himself in Muzzin's mind. One more thing for Muzzin to worry about; one more person to take into consideration while planning his final tactics. Marcus had only one tactic: to stay close to The Cannibal, then beat him on the wall. If anything unforeseen came up, he'd just have to depend on his instincts. He refused to entertain the possibility that his endurance would fail him on the final climb.

They flew down another hill, Belov shoulder to shoulder with Marcus, the pavement a gray blur beneath them. Marcus wouldn't let him in, powering ahead on the next grade, inches behind Muzzin's wheel.

The rabbits began to fall off. First McCrary and Golyadkin, then Titov, and finally Jerome. Marcus liked Jerome a lot. He hated to see him lose the pace, but it always happened. Jerome was a great team man, but he wasn't a champion. Marcus was sad that he and Jerome could no longer be friends, but Muzzin would never allow it. He required total loyalty.

"Here we go," Marcus muttered as they came down the last hill and leveled off on the brief straightaway before the wall.

"Here they come!" the promoter bellowed over the PA.

Marcus stood up and sprinted, closing to within a couple of meters of Muzzin. The Cannibal took off, and behind Marcus, Belov grunted ferociously as he made his own bid for glory.

"Ladies and gentlemen, the caravan is in sight."

Marcus tried not to listen, but the sound of the PA system was inescapable.

''They are climbing the wall, ladies and gentlemen, and in a remarkable recovery, Marcus Sommers has regained his position near the front of the lead group, after a flat tire way out on the course.''

There was no slacking off now. Marcus pulled out and gave it everything he had, his front wheel inching past Muzzin's rear.

''Ladies and gentlemen, it's Muzzin, Sommers, and the Soviet Belov fighting it out as they come up the wall. A real neck-and-neck battle as they come through. It's going to be a three-way sprint for first—the Americans Muzzin and Sommers, and the Soviet Belov. It's Muzzin first, Sommers second, and Sergei Belov of the Soviet team in third place!''

Marcus's legs were white-hot, and he felt as though someone had set a fire in his chest. Muzzin had two feet on him, then suddenly Belov was beside him, sprinting furiously. Marcus exploded with a howl, half expecting to belch fire like a dragon. He was past Belov, even with Muzzin, the finish line seconds away. Where it came from he had no idea, and for a moment he had no idea whether he was in reality or dreaming, but his body suddenly delivered a last little jolt of energy, and Marcus's bicycle shot ahead of Muzzin's and crossed the finish line.

''It's Sommers first, ladies and gentlemen! Muzzin second, and Sergei Belov in third place! What a tremendous finish! Sommers, Muzzin, and the Soviet Belov!''

Sommers, Muzzin, and Belov. He could hardly believe it. Marcus raised his arms in triumph, nearly hitting Muzzin, who rode angrily past him and disappeared into the crowd. ''You did it, buddy,'' Marcus whispered, then let out a little whoop of joy. He noticed the crowd moving toward him, and he hit the brakes and did a quick turn. ''Nice race,'' he said to Belov, who nodded wearily at him. Now to find out about David.

''Fourteen, fifteen, sixteen riders across the line,'' the announcer bawled. ''The winners are in and we are counting the other riders as they finish. Only the first forty-eight will race tomorrow.''

No sign of David. Marcus got off his bike and began to

walk, then Sarah pushed between some people and threw her arms around him. "Hey," he gasped. He was surprised he still had the strength to stand.

"That was incredible," she said.

"Not bad for a start." He kissed her on the forehead. "If you hadn't've been so fast on that tire, I'd've never made it."

"Good training," she said.

"Congratulations, Marcus," Becky said.

"Thanks, Becky. Good driving back there."

"We aim to please."

"Have you seen David?"

She shrugged. "He started the last lap in fifty-third place. I mean, fifty-fifth."

"Uh-oh." He felt too good to be terribly worried.

"Thirty-three, thirty-four, thirty-five, thirty-six."

"You think he'll make it?" Becky asked.

"Sure," Marcus said. "Let's get down there." They started for the finish line.

"You feel all right?" Sarah asked.

"Never better. What'd you put in that sandwich, anyway?"

"Secret formula." She squeezed him again.

Marcus' concern for David deepened as a couple of small packs blasted over the finish line. There weren't many slots left. He remembered some of his early races when he finished far back, out of contention. Pretty lonely feeling.

"Forty-three, forty-four, forty-five, and . . . forty-six. Only two more riders will stay in the race. The rest will have to wait for next year."

Marcus shook his head. Next year was something he couldn't afford to think about. Another big pack was starting up the wall. He thought he recognized David's blue jersey in the sea of color. Suddenly a rider in a red jersey broke out of the pack, then David was right on his wheel.

"Go, David!" Marcus bellowed. "All right!"

"Come on!" Sarah yelled.

"Ride 'em, David!" Becky took off his cowboy hat and waved it back and forth.

David swung out to the left of the other rider, pouring it

on in a concerted effort to pass. They had both put the rest of the pack far behind them. Then Red Jersey seemed to lose control; he wobbled out to the side, touched David's wheel, and they both fell over.

"Oh no!" Marcus howled. "Get up, David! Get up!"

The pack began to close as the red-jerseyed racer climbed back on his bike and broke for the finish line. David lay there for a moment, looking confused, then staggered to his feet and righted the bike. But when he climbed on, the machine wouldn't move—the front wheel was hopelessly bent.

"Run with it, David!" Marcus bellowed.

David looked at him questioningly, but already he had begun to move.

"Forty-seven!" the announcer yelled. "One more to go." Red Jersey was home free.

"Drag the thing across the finish line!" Marcus stood up and gestured furiously. "Run with it! Go! Go!" He actually started running in place, miming the dragging of a bicycle as David limped toward the finish line.

Two other riders broke out of the pack, sprinting with all they had to beat David. David kept on coming. Ten meters from the finish line he looked as if he was going to faint, then he lowered his head like a fullback on the last play of the game and lunged over the finish line, bike and all, ahead of the other racers.

"That's forty-eight, ladies and gentlemen. In a remarkable finish, David Sommers of ShaverSport has crossed the finish line as the forty-eighth and final qualifier to ride Stages Two and Three of the Hell of the West."

David fell into Marcus's arms. Marcus looked at him lovingly. "Con . . ."

"Hold it, one minute," the announcer interrupted. "We'll have to check something here about carrying a bicycle across the finish line."

David took a few deep breaths and smiled up at his big brother. "I think I screwed up."

Marcus nodded. "Well, it is a *bike* race, not a track meet."

"You were terrific," Becky said.

"The Spirit of St. Louis." Sarah smiled down at him.

Marcus helped him to his feet, and they watched expectantly as the race officials huddled together, determining David's fate. After a couple of tense moments, the head judge shrugged and nodded, and one of the lesser officials ran over to the announcer and whispered something in his ear.

"That's it, ladies and gentlemen. David Sommers of ShaverSport has been officially given the forty-eighth position in Stage One of the Hell of the West. Good luck to everyone in Stages Two and Three, and for those of you who didn't qualify, good luck next year."

"Whoo-ee!" Marcus shrieked, jumping up and down, thumping David on the back. "You did it!"

David shook his head and exhaled with relief. "You really think it was legal?"

Marcus shrugged, looking at the others. In all his years of racing, he'd never seen anything like David's finish.

"Look at it this way," Becky said. "What he did was a lot harder than riding the damn bike."

Marcus and Sarah looked at each other. "Sounds logical," Marcus said.

"It sounds *good*!" David said. He leaned back and cut loose with another coyote howl. "*Very* good, folks."

"Mr. Sommers?"

Marcus whirled, and a couple of photographers immediately snapped pictures of him. One of them pointed up past a crowd. "I think they're setting up the victory stand."

David gave him a little push. "You don't want to miss that. The yellow jersey, right?"

"Right," Marcus said. "You come with me. I want you to see this."

"I wouldn't miss it."

"Here." Sarah grabbed his bike. "You guys go ahead. I'll put this in the van, and be right with you."

"I'll take Marcus's bike," Becky said, and the girls quickly disappeared.

Marcus and David began walking toward the victory stand, Marcus pausing along the way to sign a few autographs and speak to reporters. He felt a warm glow inside; not only had he beaten Muzzin and finished first, but David had managed to hang on and qualify for the next race. So he was forty-eighth. He was still only a little more than two minutes behind the leaders. And Marcus thought he had already figured out a strategy to make up most of that time. "Those hills drop pretty fast, don't they?" he said as they approached another crowd.

"I about went off a couple of 'em," David said, mopping his brow. "But the last time around was solid."

"Good." Marcus clapped him on the back. "'Cause the next course is just as bad. Worse in places."

David shrugged. "Something to dream about." He pointed up ahead. "There's Mr. Personality now."

Muzzin was hemmed in by a group of reporters from which he was trying to escape.

"It was a real close race, wasn't it?" one of them asked.

"No shit!" Muzzin snapped.

"Could you tell us what it feels like to ride ninety miles?"

"No." Muzzin turned, looking for a way out.

A female reporter grabbed his jersey. "It's a big day for American cycling to have two Americans beat an Olympic champion. You must feel very proud."

"I'm not riding for America!" Muzzin shouted angrily. "I *tried* riding back in 1980. I spent four years working at shitty jobs so I could train and make the Olympic team and ride for America!" His face was nearly purple with rage. "Then some fat-asses in Washington started having opinions." He shook his head contemptuously and spat on the ground. "The Olympic Committee started having opinions." He stared at the reporter for a moment, then jabbed an angry finger at her. "You! You bitch, I know you."

The reporter blinked and seemed to dig her heels into the pavement. Whatever abuse she was about to get would at least be good copy. Poor Muzzin, Marcus thought. He understood the disappointment the athletes felt in 1980. But some things you put behind you graciously.

Muzzin narrowed his eyes hatefully at the reporter. "You

started writing your opinions, too. So we boycott the Olympics. I was in the best shape of my life and I got beat by opinions!'' Again he tried to push his bike out of the crowd.

''Is that why you're boycotting the victory ceremony?'' the woman said, a streetfighter herself.

''What victory?'' Muzzin whirled, briefly catching Marcus's eye, but turning right past him. ''There's two more stages to go.''

''Still,'' the woman said, ''the fact remains . . .''

''Bitch!'' Muzzin howled. ''You wouldn't know a fact if it banged you all night long.''

She had nothing to say to that one. Nor did anyone else. The crowd parted and Muzzin wheeled his bike away, full of fury and his sense of righteous indignation.

''Come on,'' Marcus said, moving toward the victory stand. So the whole race wasn't over yet. He wasn't going to let anyone take away his moment of glory. Muzzin would probably be awake half the night going over every mile of the race in his mind, trying to figure out where he screwed it up and how he could prevent it from happening again. Well, Marcus didn't blame him for that. He'd be spending some mental time himself, going over his own race and trying to figure out what Muzzin would try to do to him on Stage Two.

He stood on the victory stand and took off his ShaverSport jersey and put on the yellow jersey that would designate him as the leader in Stage Two.

''Ladies and gentlemen,'' the announcer said. ''In first place, the leader of the ShaverSport team, Marcus Sommers!''

His name seemed to echo through the mountains as Eddie Mercyx hung a medal around his neck and said, ''Congratulations, Marcus.''

''Thanks,'' Marcus whispered, shaking his hand.

The crowd cheered and applauded, and Marcus raised his arms in acknowledgment, smiling down at Sarah, David, Becky, even Jerome and Belov and some of the other riders. It was a magnificent moment, one that he would never forget.

12

David felt a little down as they drove over to the University of Colorado campus in the van, but after a shower and shave and a lumberjack's lunch, his spirits began to rise. So he hadn't done as well as he wanted to today. He'd still done pretty well, considering it was his first race. And he was still *in* the race; that's all that mattered now. He felt a surge of pride as he leaned against the railing of the sports arena's balcony, watching Marcus and Sarah down below. They were signing autographs and greeting well-wishers while a trick rider did reverse wheelies to a heavy metal beat. Marcus was in first place, and that's what David wanted anyway. He just wished he could have come a little closer. Well, tomorrow was another day.

And besides, who could remain in a bad mood for very long with Becky around? She really seemed pumped up by the race, and as impressed as hell with him, too. David shrugged, shaking his head. He guessed she didn't know too many people who carried their bikes across finish lines.

"David?"

He looked over his shoulder. Becky was holding the receiver from the pay phone and gesturing to him like crazy. This was going to be a good one, he thought, walking slowly over to the phone.

Becky gave him a devilish grin, then put the receiver to her ear. She looked terrific in the Institute T-shirt. "Hi, Mom," she said. "I'm in Colorado. . . . Sure I'm fine. Got a great tan, too. I'm with these bike riders. . . . No, not motorcycles, bicycles, bikes. You know, like the ones Daddy trips over. . . . No, they're great guys, real clean-cut. Want to say hi to one of them?" She nodded, then covered the mouthpiece of the phone. "Be nice, David, so she won't worry." She held out the phone to him.

Jesus! he thought, not knowing what to say. He felt as nervous as a tenth grader going to meet some girl's father. He cleared his throat. "Hello, Mrs. Chandler?"

"Hello." She sounded pleasant. No wonder Becky's ex-boyfriends hung around.

"How are you?" David asked.

"I'm fine," she said.

"Uh, my name is David Sommers."

"Hello, Da . . ."

But Becky grabbed the phone away from him. "Isn't he nice, Mom? . . . Well, I'm telling you, he's real nice. . . . Real smart, too. His brother's a doctor." She tugged on the T-shirt. "And David's teaching me Latin."

"Don't translate it," David whispered.

For a moment Becky covered her mouth to keep from laughing, then got serious again. "I really like him, Mom." She stared at David. "I don't know. I think he likes me, too."

He looked around nervously.

She covered the mouthpiece with her hand. "You do like me, don't you?"

He eyed her for a moment, then gave her the demented leer of a sex maniac. His cupped hands reached for her.

She began to laugh, then stuck the phone in his face.

He grabbed it. "Hello, Mrs. Chandler," he said, trying to sound as mature as possible.

"Hello, David."

"It's me again."

"I know that."

She was keeping her sense of humor, he had to give her that. "I really like Becky."

"I'm glad to hear that."

Becky lifted the T-shirt up and down, high enough for him to see, but fast enough so that he couldn't see for long.

He tried to speak, but couldn't, covering the mouthpiece instead. "Be serious," he said.

Becky flashed him again.

"I'm *crazy* about her, Mrs. Chandler."

Becky grabbed the phone away from him. "Hear that, Mom? He's crazy about me. . . . Is Dad home? . . . Well, you tell him I miss him. . . . Yeah, I love you too, Mom. . . . What? . . . Of course I'll use precaution." She gave David a challenging look. "If the need arises. 'Bye, Mom." She hung up and gave him a smile. "That should put her in a rinse cycle for the rest of the day."

"I believe so." With the phone back on the hook, he suddenly felt shy and looked at the floor.

"Hey?"

"Yeah?" He smiled sheepishly at her.

"So, you're crazy about me, huh?"

He nodded.

She smiled.

Nervous, he walked over to the balcony and looked over at the trick rider. Then she was there beside him, taking him in her arms and giving him a long, passionate kiss.

"God," he muttered. He was beginning to feel more and more happy that he'd made the trip. He looked over the balcony; Marcus and Sarah were staring up at him and Becky, applauding, and nodding their heads in approval.

They rode west into a gorgeous crimson sunset, heading for their motel. A perfect cap to a perfect day, Marcus thought. He just hoped Muzzin hadn't done anything to sabotage his room. He glanced in the rearview mirror. David and Becky were really smooching it up.

"Becky?" Marcus said.

"What's up, Doc?" she said.

"Did I ever tell you about how David learned about sex?"

"Let's see." She stroked her chin. "I believe that's been left out of the long history of our relationship."

"Well, it happened when he was ten years old."

Becky turned to David. "You lost your virginity then?"

"Marcus?" David pleaded.

"No, no, no," Marcus said. "He just started *learning* about it then. He came in my room looking all serious, see. . . ."

"Hey, come on," David said.

Becky put her hand up to his mouth. "Be quiet, will you?"

David shook his head. "Who wants to hear this stuff?"

"I do," Becky said.

"Me too." Sarah smiled back at him.

"Come on, Marcus," Becky said. "Then what happened?"

Marcus grinned. " 'What's oral sex?' he asks me."

Becky shrieked with delight and clapped her hands.

"Well," Marcus said in his best bedside manner, "I told him that oral sex is just the opposite of written sex. If you read about it, it's written sex. If you talk about it, it's oral sex."

"My brother, the doctor," David said while Becky and Sarah roared with laughter.

"Wait, wait!" Marcus said. "I'm just getting to the good part."

"I knew it," David muttered.

"Two weeks later, he goes to a birthday party for Sheila Fletcher on the third floor. Comes back in fifteen minutes. Mom and Dad want to know why he came back so quickly. 'It was boring,' David said. 'The guys were just standing around having oral sex.' "

Even David guffawed at that.

"Mom flew out of the apartment!" Marcus said, cackling like a teenager.

The van exploded with laughter, and the sound was one of the sweetest Marcus had ever heard. For a few moments, life seemed very nearly perfect. A good day's racing, an exquisite sunset, a feeling of joy among the people he loved and cared for. It couldn't get much better. As their laughter subsided, a poignant ballad came up on the radio, and everyone grew strangely silent as the van rolled on toward the motel. Marcus reached over and touched Sarah's hand and smiled, nearly overwhelmed by his bittersweet feelings and emotions. Life was too much, he thought. So incredibly strong, so infinitely fragile.

"Here we are," Becky said, pointing to the motel's marquee which read, "WELCOME TO STAGE TWO OF THE HELL OF THE WEST."

Welcome, indeed, Marcus thought.

They piled out of the van and into the lobby, greeting the other bike riders who were milling around. "Hey," he said, looking at the official result sheet that someone had thrust into his hand.

"What?" David asked.

"You're only two minutes and eleven seconds behind in the standings."

"Is that all?" David said as they walked over to the desk.

Marcus shrugged. "No big thing," he lied. A harmless lie, anyway. He shook his head as he felt a little twinge, then rubbed the back of his neck.

"How many rooms?" the clerk asked.

"One for us." Marcus nodded to Sarah. "And . . ." He stopped, then looked at David and Becky, not quite sure of what to say. He's a grownup, Marcus thought. Let him decide for himself.

David looked at Marcus for a moment, then back over his shoulder at Becky. He raised two fingers tentatively, as though he were asking her a question. She smiled and raised her index finger. David returned the smile, then turned back to the desk with a serious expression on his face. "And one for us," he said deeply.

They got their keys and started down the corridor, David and Becky moving swiftly ahead, full of anticipation. Marcus grinned at Sarah, resisting an impulse to warn David about losing the competitive edge. The kid was young and had plenty of energy. The better he felt tomorrow, the better he'd do. " 'Night," Marcus said, stopping in front of their door.

David turned and waved the key at him as though he were holding up a victory trophy.

As Marcus turned toward the door, his vision suddenly blurred, and he was unable to get the key in the slot. He rubbed his forehead and looked at Sarah, whose face seemed tense with concern. Marcus shrugged, but failed again to get the key in properly. He leaned against the door for a moment while the dizziness subsided somewhat. His vision cleared a little, and, with one hand framing the lock, he guided the key home. Let it pass, he thought. Please let it pass.

David opened the door and turned on the light, his heart pounding as though he had just sprinted ten miles with Barry Muzzin. There were two double beds in the room. David looked at Becky; she seemed a little nervous, too. She looked away, tossing her stuff on one of the beds. He threw his on the other, then walked over and turned on the television, then stared intensely at a commercial for used cars.

"You know something?" Becky said.

"What?" He couldn't turn away from the television.

"I think this whole thing was destiny."

He finally looked at her. "What whole thing?"

"This trip, you and me." She took off her sneakers. "Everything, you know what I mean?"

"I'm not sure." He slid his shoes off, too.

"There I was at a McDonald's."

"There you were."

"In the middle of Kansas."

"Western side."

"Whatever," she said. "There I was. I wanted a Quarter Pounder with cheese, okay?"

"I'm following you." The girl knew how to tell a story, he had to give her that.

"The attendant goes, 'We're out. You'll have to wait. How about a Big Mac?' "

"The world is full of these existential choices."

"Think about it," she said. "If I hadn't waited for that Quarter Pounder with cheese, I wouldn't be here with you." She walked toward him, making him more nervous.

"It's incredible to know that so much depends on a slice of beef."

"Destiny." She put her arms around him and kissed him.

"Lord," he muttered.

She kissed him again.

"Becky?"

"Huh?" she sighed, kissing his neck.

"There's something, uh, there's something you should know about me."

She leaned back suddenly, eyeing him. "Don't tell me you have a girl back home."

He shook his head. "No."

"You're not gay, are you?"

"No. Hell no. Just the opposite." He guessed that girls had to go through a lot these days. So did guys. Christ, so did everybody.

"Well?" she asked. "What is it?"

He shook his head. "I probably shouldn't be telling you this."

"It's a little late, don't you think?"

"Well, uh, you see, I think I'm going to die." It didn't sound right. The momentousness just wasn't there. He felt her lovely body relax against his.

"Thank God I'm not the only one," she said, then kissed him again.

"But . . ."

She put her finger across his lips. "I think I'm going to die if we don't do something soon." She stepped back and pointed at him as though she were an admonishing school teacher. "Don't go away." She grabbed her bag and disappeared into the bathroom.

For a moment David stood there as though someone had nailed his feet to the floor. "What the hell," he muttered finally. "I tried." In about five seconds he tore off his clothes, threw them on one bed and dove into the other. He stared at the ceiling, expecting it to open and for him to be in heaven. Then he heard the announcer saying that the TV station was going off the air. David started to pull back the covers to turn off the television, but then the bathroom door opened, so he lay back down.

Becky stepped out in her T-shirt and panties. She walked toward him, then stopped two feet from the bed and turned toward the television. A large American flag rippled in the breeze in front of a bright blue sky. "Listen," she said, a big grin on her face. "They're playing our song."

As the strains of "The Star-Spangled Banner" came up,

she wriggled out of her T-shirt and stood beside the bed. His mind a blur, David managed to remember his manners, and he calmly folded back the covers and gestured for her to come under. She slid in next to him, and the last thing he remembered thinking was that the touch of her legs against his was about the best thing he had ever felt.

13

In her dream, Sarah was chasing Marcus across a large, sun-drenched meadow, surrounded by dark, seemingly impenetrable woods. She nearly caught him, but finally he escaped into the dense forest, and for some reason that was unclear to her, she could not enter there. For several minutes she stared at the gnarled bark of an old oak tree, but it yielded nothing but the same hard truths she had heard from her embittered father. She ran laps around the meadow, crying ''Marcus! Marcus!'' until her feet bled and her breath was gone. Then she stumbled to a large rock in the middle of the clearing, sat down, and wept disconsolately.

Her eyes blinked open and she stared at the glitter-flecked ceiling of the motel room. The sun streamed through the window, and Marcus was standing there, looking out as he pulled on the yellow jersey of yesterday's victory. She looked at her watch; only six-thirty. ''Marcus?''

He turned, winced briefly, and put his hand to his forehead. ''Hi.''

''Where are you going?''

He pointed out the window. ''I want to go over the course with David.''

''No, no.'' She shook her head.

''I have to.''

''But the race isn't till noon.''

''Now's the best time.''

''It's a beautiful sunrise.''

"We'll be back before long. We can have breakfast together." He came over to the bed, bent down and kissed her. "I love you," he said.

"I love you, too."

"I'll see you in a bit." He started to leave.

"Marcus?"

He turned at the door and looked at her.

"You all right?"

He forced a wink. "I'll be fine." Then he was gone.

They both knew better, Sarah thought, sitting up in bed and wrapping her arms around her knees. They hadn't talked about it last night, choosing instead to make slow and tender love. Marcus had fallen asleep soon afterwards, and the last thing Sarah wanted to do was wake him up. He'd talk when he was ready; she wasn't going to push him. Still, there were other things that had to be done.

As Marcus drove the van up one of the steeper hills of Stage Two, he was riding the race in his mind, trying to crowd out everything else. His headache was gone, and maybe, after all, it had been nothing more than that—a simple headache. He knew better. But then again, maybe he wouldn't have another one for months. He knew better.

"Wow!" David said, looking down the steep precipice at the right of the road. "I guess you're a goner if you go off there."

"This is true," Marcus said. "So don't get drunk before the race, okay?"

"If you insist."

Marcus was grateful for David's lightheadedness this morning. The boy had obviously had a pleasant night. Marcus just hoped he could concentrate on the race when the time came. He stopped the van at the top of the hill where a yellow flag had been planted on the side of the road. "Come on." He got out.

David followed him, adjusting his cowboy hat. He let go with a coyote yell that echoed back to them. "Good acoustics," he said.

"Hey, let's have a rock concert." Marcus pointed to the yellow flag. "Now, there'll be four of these flags scattered around the course. Each one will be on a hilltop. Whoever crosses it first gains thirty seconds on his time."

David nodded vaguely.

"You understand?" Marcus asked.

David chucked a small rock down the gorge. "I'm not an idiot, you know?"

"I know," Marcus said. "But today I want you to ride like an idiot."

"I thought I did that yesterday."

"Come on." They got back in the van and drove on to the next flag.

"Nice scenery up here," David said.

"I know, I know." Marcus was getting a little impatient. David didn't seem serious enough about the race. "But I want you to forget about the scenery today."

"And race like an idiot." David gave him an idiotic smile.

Marcus shook his head and pointed at the next flag. "Here's what I mean. You're two minutes and eleven seconds behind. Because nobody knows you, if you do something stupid like take off by yourself, they'll let you go."

"I sound like a real threat."

"It's a way to get back some of the time you lost."

"You stay up all night thinking this up?"

Maybe he *had* been getting too heavy. "I had better things to do last night, David. I think you did, too."

David looked out the window and sighed.

"But today's the race, and that's what we concentrate on now."

"What's the big deal, Marcus?" David turned and faced him. "You're winning. You don't need me."

Marcus stopped the van and put his hand on David's shoulder. "The big deal is that you're my brother."

David eyed him for a moment, then turned away.

"Got it?" Marcus asked.

"Got it," David muttered.

Dennis Conrad took the call from Sarah in the activity room, but he could hardly hear her for the crashing equipment and groaning athletes. "I'm putting you on hold, Sarah. I'll pick it up in the office."

"Okay," she said.

He punched the hold button and hung up the receiver, then pointed a stern, fatherly finger at his son, Randolph, who had just planted his buttocks in a rowing machine. "You keep at it now, you hear?"

"Sure, Dad." Randolph grinned, a liar's grin if ever there was one.

Shaking his head, Dennis ran to the office and picked up the phone. "Sarah?"

"Hi."

"Good to hear you. How's it goin'? How's Marcus?"

"He won the first stage, Denny."

"That's great!"

"You should've seen him." The pride in her voice was palpable.

"I wish I could've, but the son of a bitch told me I couldn't come. He didn't want me there."

"I know you understand that."

"Yeah." He didn't like to think of Marcus's illness. "So he did it, huh?"

"He did." She paused, and suddenly Dennis felt a chill come over the line. Involuntarily, his whole body shook. "Denny," Sarah said, "I think it's begun."

"Oh, man," he gasped. For a moment neither of them said anything, then Dennis asked, "Bad?"

"I think it's just some twinges and a headache."

"Ugh." That was the beginning. Unfortunately, Berry aneurysm had a fast beginning.

"We haven't even talked about it," Sarah said. "He's out on the course with David right now."

"Jesus!" Dennis wiped his forehead wearily. "I don't suppose he'd consider not racing today."

"Never."

"Hardhead." He tried to consider the situation logically. "Does David know?"

"I don't think so."

"Sarah, I know Marcus is against it, but I was thinking about his mother."

"Yeah?"

"Well, somebody ought to tell her."

"I've never talked to her, Denny. I don't think she knows I exist."

"I told her."

"*You* told her?"

"She called here a few days ago. I don't know why."

"So *you've* talked to her."

"That's right." He paused, stroking his chin. "I guess that puts it on me, huh?"

"I don't know if I could talk to her, Denny."

"I understand. I'll take care of it."

"I appreciate it."

"Sarah?"

"Yeah?"

"Is there anything else I can do?"

"I wish there was," she said. "I wish there was something *I* could do."

"I know what you mean. Listen, call me right away if there're any changes."

"I will, Denny. Thanks."

"Be strong, kid."

"'Bye."

The phone clicked dead, and Dennis just sat there for a moment, staring at it. "Shit," he muttered, slamming the receiver home. Why Marcus, of all people? No more dumb-ass questions, he thought. No questions, period. For the first time in years—possibly decades—he wept.

"Phew!"

Dennis wiped his eyes quickly as his son pushed through the door.

"I had a bitch of a workout, Dad."

Dennis looked up and nodded at his son.

Randolph could obviously see that he had been crying, and immediately came over to him, a look of concern on his face. "You okay, Dad?"

"No," Dennis said. He thought it was the first time he had ever answered that particular question negatively.

Randolph slapped him on the back. ''Come on, cheer up. It's not your fault.''

''I know,'' he said sadly.

Randolph shrugged. ''Every black man can't have a son who's Julius Erving.''

Strangely touched by Randolph's explanation, Dennis reached out and hugged him. After a moment he drew back and looked at Randolph's sweatshirt. ''You're soaking wet.''

Randolph looked away. ''Sweat.''

''Funny,'' Dennis said. ''Doesn't smell like sweat.''

''I used a deodorant.'' He grinned at his father. The liar's grin again.

And probably soaked yourself at the drinking fountain, Dennis thought. ''Go take a shower then.'' He wasn't going to deal with it today. ''I have a phone call to make.'' He gave Randolph a kiss on the cheek, then pushed him toward the door.

When his son was gone, Dennis bent over the phone stared at it, shaking his head. How the hell was he going to handle this one?

14

Physically, Marcus felt like going back to bed, but there was no way in hell he was going to back out of this race so long as he could sit in the saddle and pump his legs around. He jumped into the lead right away, David on his wheel, and they stayed that way for the first few miles. The day was beastly hot, miragelike heat puddles lying all over the road and gelatinous vapors shimmering in the air. It was not a day for careless riding, and there were moments when he questioned the strategy he had devised for the race. But there was no changing it now. Besides, he thought David would have sense enough to control himself. It was going to be an interesting race.

He bounced across the tracks into the Monument, the pace vehicle flashing its red lights and letting loose with a long wail on its siren. Marcus glanced at the spectators in their protective hats and dark glasses. This was where the race really began. He ran his hand across his forehead and wiped the sweat on his jersey.

"Ladies and gentlemen," the announcer said. "One look at the lunarscape of the spectacular Colorado National Monument and you understand why it has come to be known as the Tour of the Moon. The view and terrain are like nothing on earth, with bright red rock formations, tunnels, numerous sheer cliff drop-offs and rapid descents. This race is a grueling eighty-three miles."

Tell me about it, Marcus thought, looking up at the steep switchbacks as Muzzin and Jerome sprinted past him. He looked back at David and shook his head. Not time yet. But he speeded up enough so that Muzzin didn't get much more than ten meters beyond him.

After a few minutes they approached an immense conical rock that he had designated as a marker that morning. He looked back over his shoulder, noticing that a few of the laggards from Stage One had passed the Sunnino team and looked like they were going to make a move. Marcus nodded to David and pointed his finger to the top of the mountain.

David nodded back, took a deep breath and suddenly took off, standing up and sprinting past Marcus.

Marcus let him get a few meters ahead, then stood up and sprinted himself, faking a chase. They blew past Jerome, and after he'd gotten a few meters beyond Muzzin, Marcus yelled, "David, don't be a fool."

But David continued to sprint, following their script to the letter. Marcus gave up the chase, slowing down enough so that he kept a short lead on Muzzin. Then three riders he didn't know zipped past him, giving chase to David.

"They're nobodies," Muzzin gasped to Jerome. "Let them go."

Marcus looked back over his shoulder.

"They'll die," Muzzin said, supremely confident.

Marcus's hand went involuntarily to his head, but he quickly grabbed the handlebars again, gritted his teeth and surged forward. The dull throb in his head was only a nuisance; it wasn't doing anything to slow him down.

Still, he tried to keep the pace just a little slow without being obvious, continually checking up ahead as David and the other three riders pulled away. He saw the yellow flag rippling in the distance. "Come on, David," he whispered. The three other riders didn't seem to be fading away. David was going to have to work to get this one.

"Here they come up the hill now, ladies and gentlemen. The first rider past the flag will gain thirty seconds on his time. Here comes number seven, Uli, of the Kelley team, starting a sprint from the rear of the breakaway group."

Marcus shook his head as he watched Uli go by David. "Come on!" he muttered, suddenly furious at the thought of how he had lost last year to Muzzin. "Come on!"

"But here comes David Sommers of ShaverSport. It looks like these two are both going for that thirty seconds. Uli is in the lead, but Sommers is coming up hard abreast. They're right up to the flag, and it's Sommers who wins that very valuable time advantage!"

Marcus let out a sigh of relief, almost losing his concentration as the grade increased. He took a deep breath and forged on as David and the others dipped out of sight over the crest.

He had to fight every inch of the way to the top of the switchback, but he kept fighting, never giving in to his desire to slow down and rest his weary body. Even when they had crested the hill, he shifted and got up to maximum speed on the hellish descent before he stopped pedaling and let his leg muscles regroup. He wasn't going to give up until someone put a brick wall in front of him.

For all the times he had made the Tour of the Moon, Marcus never lost his awe of the terrain. Riding up the hills stressed the endurance of the *best* athlete, and riding down required consummate skill and intelligence. Coming down was slightly cooler, but the coolness was only relative—the wind still bore a faint resemblance to a blast furnace. And on one side of the road, jagged rocks that would mangle your bike and tear your body to shreds; on the other, sheer drops that no one could survive without a parachute. Still, the beauty was so phenomenal that to experience it like this was worth whatever pain was necessary. He felt truly blessed to be here.

Suddenly things darkened as he led the chase group into a tunnel that had been blasted out of the mountain. It was a little cooler in here, but nothing you'd compare to a Wisconsin winter.

Out into the sunlight again, he looked over his shoulder and noticed Muzzin tensing up. Ahead, David and his group of nobodies was widening its lead as they headed for the next yellow flag. Even Marcus was surprised that they'd been able to go so hard so long.

"Jerome!" Muzzin bellowed. "Let's reel those creeps in!"

The voice had authority, and within a minute Jerome, Muzzin and the two blond rabbits sprinted past Marcus. Then came the Russians and the Japanese. Hurting, Marcus pursued, drafting off the Sunnino team.

"Ladies and gentlemen, they're coming up to the second flag now, and the breakaway group looks like they're starting to run out of gas. David Sommers is going to try to take this flag as well. He's got it! And the way the chase group is coming up on his heels, he'll need all the time advantage he can get."

"All right!" Marcus said, causing Yamashita to look over his shoulder at him. Marcus smiled, and with a sudden burst of energy, swung out and passed. He got by the rest of the Japanese team going up, pulling up behind the Russians on a steep, curving descent.

They flew along a brief straightaway, Muzzin setting a blistering pace. Marcus drafted off of Golyadkin as they raced through another tunnel.

"We got 'em!" Muzzin said triumphantly as they came into the sunlight.

Marcus looked up. He couldn't tell if it was the sun or

something worse, but his vision seemed blurred. It looked like four riders disappearing around a curve twenty-five meters ahead of them.

He stayed on Golyadkin's wheel, fighting momentary spasms of dizziness. He looked back once, seeing the van come around a curve, then faced forward and passed the first of the exhausted riders from the breakaway group. Too bad, Marcus thought, thinking that his whole strategy had gone down the drain. Well, he couldn't blame David. With this heat and his inexperience, he'd have to be Superman *not* to fold up. They went past Uli, and in another thirty seconds they passed the red-jerseyed racer who had collided with David yesterday. David would be next.

The Russians began babbling about something Marcus couldn't understand. Muzzin looked around, then said to Jerome, "Where the hell's the other one?"

For a moment, nothing dawned on Marcus, then he suddenly became very alert. He looked around quickly but saw no David. He felt another twinge in his head, then he had the horrible thought that David hadn't been able to handle the last descent and had plunged off the road to his death.

They roared around another turn and started up a hill. Marcus looked halfway up. Nothing. Then a little farther. "Jesus Christ!" he said, breaking into a broad grin. Near the top of the hill, flying along a switchback nearly a mile ahead of them, was someone in a blue jersey. He knew only one person in a blue jersey in this race. What the hell had the kid done? Fastened a rocket to his bike? Whatever he'd done, Marcus wasn't going to question it now.

He faced forward and caught Muzzin glaring over his shoulder at him. "I taught you that move, Marcus."

Marcus nodded, giving The Cannibal his best smile.

"Son of a bitch!" Muzzin said, facing front. "Jerome!"

Jerome stood up and shot past Muzzin.

Marcus didn't even need to think about it. Suddenly he found himself on the outside of Golyadkin, then just as suddenly he put the whole Russian team behind him. Standing up, pumping furiously, he rolled past McCrary, then past the amazed Muzzin, then Jerome was behind him, too.

Marcus Sommers was climbing the hill like a demon, chasing after his brother.

He sprinted like a machine that had been programmed not to quit, ignoring one level of fatigue, pushing through another, transcending a third. For a few ineffable moments he knew deep in his bones that he had never ridden this well, that no one ever had. Muzzin was fifty meters behind him, giving it his best, No way, Marcus thought. You can't touch me now.

Then he saw the blood. Just a drop on his jersey, a scarlet stain against the yellow badge of victory. His lip felt moist with more than sweat. Another drop hit his jersey, a third dropped on his thigh. He made a quick swipe across his nose with his glove, the blood making the dull black leather shine. He still felt fine, and continued pumping madly toward the top of the hill. David had crested the hill now, disappeared. Marcus pulled out his water bottle and squirted a few drops on his nose, then doused his head and put the bottle back in its cage. He took another deep breath and surged on to the top of the hill, desperately trying to keep his hopes alive.

They deserted him as he started down the next breathtaking descent. Something snapped inside his head—he thought that he heard a little ping—severing forever his normal connection to the world. For a moment the lights went out entirely, then suddenly came back on, but his clarity had been obscured by fog. "Oh, no!" he moaned, wobbling a little, but managing to stay upright. It was over, there was no disputing that. All that remained was to get himself out of this without hurting himself or anyone else.

His reactions felt like they were no quicker than a sloth's. He managed to touch the handbrake with one hand, raising the other and moving to the side so the other riders would know he was out of action. Everything was a blur. He was going too fast. He wanted to savor the lead he had built up over the others, but that too was gone in a moment. Muzzin sped by him, glancing at Marcus with a look of concern. Marcus looked away as more blood dripped on to his yellow jersey. Then the others went by—McCrary, Jerome, Belov, Golyadkin. Marcus closed his eyes for a moment, weaving across the road, then the sound of the van's horn brought him back to reality. He tried to grab the brakes, but his hands simply wouldn't move.

Sarah's stomach fell as she saw Marcus veer off the line and begin to slow down. Instinctively she looked at his tires and his chain, then a sadder instinct took over and she simply shook her head. She had no way of fixing what was going wrong. It pained her to watch the other bikes tear remorselessly past Marcus's. The race must go on, she thought, knowing that Marcus would be thinking the same thing.

She expected him to pull to the side of the road and stop, but he didn't, and as he began weaving down the descent, she realized that he was out of control. Sarah let out a little scream.

"What's the matter? Becky asked, popping up from the low position she had taken to avoid looking over the precipices.

Sarah said nothing, shaking her head, gritting her teeth and trying to get hold of herself. She accelerated, getting as close behind him as she could. He moved toward the edge, then back again toward the wall of rocks on the right side of the road.

"Oh no!" Becky moaned.

Sarah stayed right behind him as he wobbled like a drunkard down the hill. She felt at once totally helpless and utterly determined to save him. She saw blood dripping from his nose and one of his ears. She gripped the steering wheel so hard that the muscles in her forearms bunched up in knots. Marcus's hands seemed to be reaching futilely for his handbrakes. He veered to the right again, nearly colliding with the wall, then started back to the left. Sarah had to do something *now*!

Treating the van as though it were a sports car, she shot in between Marcus and the rocks, steering with one hand and reaching out the window with the other and grabbing his right arm. She touched the brake lightly, then realized she was going to lose him. "Becky!" she howled. "Take the wheel!"

"I got it!" Becky slid over and put both hands on the right side of the steering wheel.

Just as Marcus was about to slip out of her grasp, Sarah got her right hand out the window and clamped down on his arm. She had him! He looked at her dumbly, his mind seemingly unable to process what was going on. Sarah literally hung on for dear life, applying steady pressure to the brakes until the van finally came to a halt at the bottom of the hill. Sarah looked at Becky and smiled gratefully. "Thanks."

Becky exhaled with relief, nodding her head. For once, she seemed speechless.

Marcus simply leaned against the van like an exhausted rider taking a break. Sarah kept hold of him with one hand and caressed his cheek with the other. The absurd thing was that there was no way for her to open the door.

"I'll get him." Becky put the van in Park, turned off the ignition and set the emergency brake, then she jumped out and ran around the van to steady Marcus while Sarah got out.

Sarah quickly undid his toestraps, then the two women got him off the bike. He leaned against the van, breathing heavily, still not quite aware of what was going on.

"Sarah," Becky said, panic beginning to set in, "what happened to him?"

"He's sick." Sarah grabbed a handkerchief and wiped away the blood beneath his nose and ear.

"Is he going to be all right?"

Sarah turned to Becky and put her finger to her lips. "Shh." She took off Marcus's helmet and poured a little water on his head, then wiped him with a towel.

"I'll put the bike away." Becky wheeled the machine around to the rear of the van and put it in.

Gradually the light came back into Marcus's eyes, and he stared intensely at Sarah, then shook his head and blinked a couple of times. "Hi."

"How you doin'?" She kissed him on the cheek.

He looked around as a pack of riders raced past them. "I've been better." He shrugged.

"You'll be fine."

He gave her a skeptical look.

"Becky!" Sarah called, putting her arm around Marcus.

"Yeah?" Becky returned form the rear of the van, trying to look as nonchalant as possible.

"Help me get Marcus in the back seat."

"Sure." Becky smiled. "Hi, Marcus."

"Hi," he muttered.

The women helped him around to the other side of the van and up into the rear seat. "Would you mind driving, Becky?" Sarah asked, sitting down and cradling Marcus in her arms.

"Not at all."

"I think we better get back to the motel."

Marcus nodded forlornly.

"Okay," Becky said cheerfully. She hopped in the front seat, fired up the van, and drove away.

They rode in silence a while, passing most of the racers. Sarah stroked Marcus who breathed heavily, as though he were laboring under a great weariness. From a glance in the rear view mirror, Sarah saw that Becky was crying quietly.

Marcus seemed to perk up a bit as the van cruised by the main chase group. Sunnino, Gita, the Russians, and finally Muzzin and the Seven-Eleven team all disappeared to the rear of the van. Marcus looked perplexed. "Where's David?" he asked.

Becky pointed out the front window. "Up ahead," she sniffed, then wiped her tears and turned around and smiled.

"All right!" Marcus actually managed a smile and a little laugh. Sarah squeezed him lovingly.

The van cruised past David, and Sarah couldn't tell if he had seen them or not. She waved, but he stared straight ahead, looking more like a zombie than a human being. She hoped he could keep his lead, but right now the important thing was to get Marcus back to the motel room. They drove on through the last few miles of the course, past all the spectators lining the road on the way to the finish line. She felt especially sad for Marcus when they rolled over the line itself. If they could have gotten out another way, she surely would have taken it. He gave a resigned look to the race officials in their booth, then gave himself over to the comfort of Sarah's arms.

15

After he had taken the second yellow flag and the other three riders in the breakaway group had fallen off, David seemed to drift into some otherworldly state where he was at once anchored in reality and completely cut adrift. His bike and the road were real; his bike moved, the road didn't. The heat and the fatigue had ceased to present any physical impediment to what he was doing, pushing him instead into a swirling world where road signs jumped out and hitchhiked in front of him and huge rocks rotated like the turrets on Army tanks. He had considered stopping but decided to forge ahead. There was only one bike and one road, and they were doing what they were supposed to do. Part of him knew that the other sideshow was unreal; as long as he could differentiate, why not keep racing? He guessed that he wouldn't know when the time arrived that he could no longer differentiate, but he decided to take the gamble.

He barely noticed when he blasted by the third yellow flag, and he felt virtually no fear as he flew down one of the incredibly steep hills. The descents were a lot easier when he was by himself. He slid into the mental mode of his training sessions back in St. Louis, setting a blistering pace and putting world champions to shame.

He took the fourth yellow flag in fine style, then people began appearing at the sides of the highway, clapping and cheering him on. His own team van went by, and suddenly he realized that he *was* in a race with several world champions (or at least contenders), and that if he was where he thought he was, he *was* putting them to shame. The realization caused him to gasp for breath and reach for his water bottle. Acknowledging reality caused his body to acknowledge the heat and pain and fatigue, and for a moment he thought he might have to stop. "No way," he muttered, spraying his head with water. Not with his big brother watching.

He took a quick glance over his shoulder. No Marcus. Muzzin and Belov were back there, chasing him as though they were the police. But no Marcus. What the hell was happening? He had fulfilled his part of the game plan, but Marcus was supposed to come roaring on and win the goddamn race. He looked back again. Still no Marcus. But Muzzin and Belov were gaining. Hell with it, David thought. No more looking back. No more doing anything but giving it all you've got.

Everything was completely real now, and he flew down the road toward the finish line. Over the cheers and exhortations of the tightly packed spectators, he could hear Muzzin and Belov grunting as they closed the gap.

"Ladies and gentlemen," the PA boomed, "they're coming down to the finish line and David Sommers is still in the lead. But the chase group is breathing down his neck and getting closer every second. . . . Here they come, David Sommers still in the lead. Barry Muzzin and the Russian are coming fast. . . . And they've got him! David Sommers has been swallowed up by the chase group! . . . Here they go, and now Belov is starting a devastating sprint of his own. . . . Here they come down to the line. Belov, Muzzin, and Sommers. . . . It's Muzzin and Belov! And it's Barry Muzzin finishing first, Belov second, and David Sommers third. Oh my! What a race!"

David's lungs nearly exploded as he raced over the finish line, sucking Belov's wheel. He barely had the strength to reach for his hand brakes, and he thought his heart was going to leap out of his chest. He finally stopped, undid his toestraps, and climbed off his bike. He took a cup of water from someone and drank greedily, stopping because he needed air. His legs felt like soggy noodles, and he moved over and leaned against a table so he wouldn't fall down. People slapped him on the back and offered congratulations, but he barely noticed. Off to the side, Muzzin had his arms raised in victory, his fists clenched, and he was screaming like an animal.

In a few moments David got his bearings and immediately began to look for Marcus. At least twenty racers had now crossed the finish line, but David's big brother was not among them. What could have happened? Slowly, David wheeled his bike toward the finish line. Six more riders came in.

"David!"

He looked over his shoulder and saw Becky pushing her way through the crowd. "Becky!" He started toward her. "Where's Marcus?"

They came together in the midst of a sea of people. Becky's face was streaked with tears, and he had never seen her look this sad. He didn't think she could even *feel* sad. "What's wrong?" David asked. "Where's Marcus?"

"Come on." She began leading him out of the crowd.

"What's the matter?"

"He's sick, David. I don't know. He got all disoriented and had to stop in the middle of the race."

"Where is he?"

"Back at the motel. He had a nosebleed, and it was coming out his ears, too."

"Oh, no," David whispered, stopping and shaking his head. "Oh, no."

Becky grabbed his hand and tugged. "Come on," she said. "We better go."

The van hadn't even stopped in the motel parking lot before David had jumped out. He ran into the building, down the hall, and burst through the door of Marcus's room. His brother was sitting on the bed, Sarah's arm around him. He looked alert, but physically debilitated, almost as if he had shrunk an inch or two. David didn't know what to think. Part of him had expected Marcus to be in much worse condition; part of him didn't believe that anything at all was wrong.

"Hi," Marcus said, smiling.

"Uh, hi."

After a moment, Marcus said, "So, how much time did you make up?"

The question stunned David. "Two minutes."

"Really?"

"Yeah."

"Great!" Marcus clenched his fist victoriously. "We did it. You did it, huh?"

David nodded, fighting back tears at the sight of so much joy in Marcus's face. He noticed the bloody towel next to him on the bed. "Marcus?"

"Yeah?" Marcus sniffed and shook his head, wincing with pain.

"What the hell is going on?"

Sarah moved her arm out from behind him, then eased him back against the pillows. She walked past David without a word and left the room, closing the door behind herself.

The silence was so thick that David thought he could float in it. Finally Marcus looked at him and shrugged. "I told you that you were fine—free of disease—didn't I?"

David nodded. "Sure you told me. But . . ."

"Nobody asked."

David tossed his head back as though someone had slapped him. "You bastard," he said. "How am I supposed to . . ."

"All right. All right!" Marcus said. "Look, I wanted you to come with me. You remember, the two of us. The Sommers team."

"Yeah?"

"Yeah," Marcus said.

"And did it ever occur to you that you could've told me? That maybe, just maybe, I'd come through for you? How many goddamn brothers do you think I have, you son of a bitch?"

Marcus managed a little laugh. "It's a good thing you dropped out of pre-med, David. Your bedside manner is atrocious."

"How can you be sick?" David snapped, fighting back tears. "I mean, look at you. You have a mustache, and all. . . ." He stopped for a moment. He had never felt so confused in all his life. "You see, I had it all figured out. You know. How to handle it, if it's me. But not you." He shook his head wearily. "I don't know what to feel, Marcus."

"You feel what you feel."

David pulled out the chair from the desk and sat in it backwards, resting his arms on the top. "I mean, am I supposed to feel glad it's you and not me, is that what?" At this point, the fact that he was going to live didn't do a thing for him.

Marcus stared at him for a moment, then looked down at the bedspread. David was going to have to work out his feelings on his own.

Sarah walked slowly across the motel parking lot, head down, arms folded beneath her breasts, kicking an empty beer can along in front of her.

"Sarah?"

She looked up to see Muzzin standing beside his van. He had just snapped off the front wheel of his bicycle and was getting ready to load up and move on to Stage Three.

"Hi, Barry," she said.

Jerome looked at them nervously, as though he were mentally preparing for another fight.

"What happened to Marcus?" Muzzin asked. His tone was neutral, almost concerned.

Sarah looked at him sadly. "He had some trouble."

Muzzin nodded. "I hope he feels better, Geronimo."

She gave him a little smile. "Thanks, Cannibal." She bent her head and began to walk away.

"Muzzin," Jerome said, "you all right?"

"Sure," Muzzin said. "Why?"

"You sounded half human."

Sarah stopped, waiting for Muzzin's reply.

"I am half human," he said after a moment.

She smiled and continued on to the van. She had to do something with Becky. All of this was too much for the poor girl.

Becky came around the van before Sarah got there and walked right up to her, looking very determined.

"Becky," Sarah said, "I was just . . ."

"Listen, Sarah," Becky interrupted.

"Yeah?"

"I just wanted to tell you, uh, to be real strong now, okay?"

As Sarah began to nod, Becky brought her hand out from behind her back. It held the rock with which Sarah had threatened Muzzin. The gesture touched Sarah deeply. She tried to say something, but the sight of the silly rock and the generous sincerity of Becky's face undid her completely. Her body shuddered as the first tears rolled down her cheeks, then she wrapped her arms around Becky and buried her face in her shoulder. Then she let herself go completely and wept and wept, while Becky held her and stroked her hair.

David went over the sequence of events with Marcus, his early fears that he had inherited their father's fatal illness, fears that were only heightened by Marcus's coming to St. Louis and taking him to Wisconsin. Then there was the CAT scan and his misinterpreting the conversation between Marcus and Dennis Conrad that he'd overheard. It was stupid, but it had never entered his mind that Marcus could be sick. David hoped that talking about it would objectify the issue somewhat, make it easier to understand and deal with. But it didn't. And as the objective fact that his brother was going to die really took hold of him, he could think of absolutely nothing to say. He hung his head over the back of the chair and stared sadly at the carpet.

"Hey," Marcus said after a few moments.

"Yeah?" David couldn't bring himself to look up.

"You still have to finish the race."

For a moment, David couldn't believe what he was hearing. "You're crazy, you know that?" He looked at Marcus and shook his head. "I think you've eaten too many bananas." He instantly felt ashamed; maybe the disease was affecting Marcus's rationality, too.

Marcus smiled at him, then dabbed a little blood away from his nose. "It's not over."

"It's over for me." David threw up his hands. "Don't you understand?"

"Understand what?"

"That the race doesn't matter now. It's you."

Marcus looked at David as though he were a child. "Is that right?"

"That's right," David said emphatically.

Marcus dabbed at his nose again. "And what're you going to do for me?"

David stood up and began to pace, feeling close to useless. "I don't know."

"That's a start."

"We'll take you to a hospital."

Marcus shook his head sadly. "David, I don't know how much time I've got left. Maybe a few days, maybe more, but basically there's really nothing they can do for me."

David put out his hands as though they could ward off the truth.

"I'm not trying to be a hero," Marcus said, "but I'm not gonna let them make me into a chef's salad either, so you're not taking me anywhere."

"You sure?" he muttered.

"I'm a doctor, David. And I know more about this disease than you'll ever know. Believe me, there's nothing anyone can do."

"Then I'll stay here with you, but I'm not racing tomorrow."

Marcus gave him a disapproving look. "That's just great," he said. "And then years from now, you can tell your kids, 'Oh, there was this big bike race in Colorado, and I could've done great if it weren't for my brother.'" Marcus exhaled angrily. "You're not going to use me as an excuse!"

"I'm not listening to this anymore."

"I'm still alive, goddammit! So don't you dare ignore me!"

"I'm sorry." David looked to the ceiling for help. "I didn't mean it like that. All of this is just too much for me."

"It's too much for me, too!" Marcus paused, letting the news sink in.

"I'm sorry," David whispered again.

Marcus shrugged. "The thing is, David, we have a tradition in our family. We fall apart in crises. Don't you think it's time we start a new tradition?"

For a moment, David bristled, thinking that Marcus was going to start in on their mother again. But then the truth hammered him like a pile driver. He was so overcome with emotion at the thought of what Marcus had done yesterday and what he had tried to do today, that he had to turn and face the wall. He stared at a ridiculous painting of two children playing in a bed of tulips, trying to get control of himself so he could talk.

"David?" Marcus said after a few moments.

He faced him. "Yeah?"

"You all right?"

David nodded, walking toward the bed. "You know how I was in your office when I heard you and Dr. Conrad next door. . . ."

"I know," Marcus interrupted impatiently. "You told me all that."

"Do you remember what you told him?"

"Oh, come on, David. We went over this already." Marcus shook his head as though he were in pain. "I'm sorry you misunderstood, but . . ."

David held up his hand to stop him. " 'I don't want to ruin it for him,' you said. 'I love him too much for that.' You remember now?"

"No." Marcus seemed embarrassed, and he looked away. "Maybe I do."

David suddenly felt stronger than he had ever felt in his life. "Well, I swore to myself that sooner or later I'd say it to your face." He came over and sat down on the bed.

Marcus continued to look at the wall.

"You have to look at me," David said.

For a moment, Marcus seemed frozen, then slowly he turned toward David. "We're going to do it the hard way, huh?"

"I love you, too, Marcus." He bit his lip to hold back the tears, then reached out and hugged his brother.

They stayed that way for nearly a minute, finally drawing back when Sarah and Becky came into the room.

"Hi," David said.

Sarah nodded at them both, seeming to sense the emotion in the room. After a moment, she said, "What's the plan?"

Marcus kept his head bowed, too moved to answer.

David smiled. "Stage Three," he said proudly, a shiver going down his spine as Marcus reached out and touched his arm.

16

"Ladies and gentlemen, prior to the start of the third and final stage of the race they call the Hell of the West, we would like to introduce you to the main contenders in this competition. Beginning with the rider in third place overall, eleven seconds behind the leader, David Sommers . . . In second place overall, from the Soviet Union, only two seconds behind the leader, Sergei Belov . . . And, ladies and gentlemen, last year's winner of the Hell of the West, the race leader today going into the third and final stage, Barry, The Cannibal, *Muzzin*!"

It was a beautiful day in Golden, Colorado, and although he was sitting in the van with barely enough energy to support himself, Marcus couldn't remember being so excited at the start of a race. He watched David sit calmly in the front row of racers while Belov raised his hands and Muzzin blew mocking kisses at the Russians. Marcus could tell that it was going to be a good race. He and David had worked out no grand strategy. His younger brother was simply to stay close to the leaders and worry them a little, then bust their chops on the sprint to the finish.

"Ladies and gentlemen, we are just minutes from the start of the competition. All caravan drivers please report to your vehicles. All officials please report to your vehicles. . . . Ann Navara, Ann Navara. Please go to the timer's booth. Mr. Greenberg, please meet Andy at the starting line."

There was a protracted roar as the engines of the myriad vehicles came to life. A radio helicopter detached from the earth and screwed its way into the sky. Sarah looked over at

Marcus. He gave her the thumbs up, and she started the engine and turned the trip odometer back to zero. As she opened her mouth to say something, Becky, sitting between them, said, "Here we go." She clapped her hands excitedly.

Marcus watched the starter raise his gun, fighting another wave of sadness as it washed over him. He thought he had set his mind at ease last night, but he knew there was no way of escaping the pain of not being out there. To hell with it, he thought. He admonished himself to watch the race and enjoy it as much as possible. The gun sounded and the riders took off. "Go get 'em, David!" Marcus yelled, brandishing his fist out the window.

"All right!" Becky said.

Marcus looked at Sarah and pointed straight ahead. "Let's go," he said.

"Roger." She saluted him, put the van in gear, and started after the racers.

"Let's stay as close to David as we can."

Sarah nodded. "I got it under control."

Marcus watched for a few minutes while the line began to take shape, then suddenly the red-jerseyed Russians surged out ahead of the pack. "Jesus," he muttered, doubting the wisdom of their move. He turned on the radio and fiddled with the dial until he got the race broadcast.

"The Russians have started an early breakaway, right in the middle of the town of Golden. They may be hoping to force the pace early on and drop the weaker cyclists who won't be able to make the grueling climbs yet to come."

Marcus winced, thinking of some of those climbs.

"Can they do that?" Becky asked.

"They can try," Marcus said. "If they can get someone to make a mistake, they'll be in good shape."

"So long as they aren't making one," Sarah said.

"Belov's tough," Marcus said. "He could probably ride across Siberia without taking a leak."

"His booty might get a little sore," Becky said.

Marcus shook his head. "His booty's made out of shoe leather." He pointed ahead. "Look at that." The Sunnino team caught the Russians, then blasted by them. Then David took off after them. When David got ten meters ahead of the Seven-Eleven team, Muzzin pointed to Jerome, and Jerome began chasing David. Muzzin was too smart to be fooled two days in a row. Marcus turned up the volume on the radio again.

"Ladies and gentlemen, the Golden to Mount Evans race is the third and final stage of the Hell of the West, and it is also the most difficult. It starts at the Coors Brewery in Golden, Colorado, and begins a spectacular climb over six thousand feet into the Rocky Mountains, finishing nearly twelve thousand feet above sea level. It goes over the highest paved road here in North America. Not many of these cyclists have ever been this high or at this altitude, since the European courses through the Alps are much, much lower. Its a torturous course, and even the most powerful cyclist cannot get enought air to maintain his normal speed."

"It's a bitch," Marcus said, turning the volume down again. "The first time I went up there I thought someone was jabbing knives into my lungs."

"Sounds like a lot of laughs," Becky said. "You think David'll make it?"

"Sure," Marcus said confidently, hoping with all his might that the altitude wouldn't be too much for his brother. "He's going to win the race."

Sarah looked over at him and raised her eyebrows.

"He is," Marcus said. "Don't worry."

David Sommers had begun Stage Three of the Hell of the West with just one thought in mind—to win. To win for his brother, or for his mother, or the memory of his father, or Becky, or Sarah, or the winos who taunted him from the East St. Louis housing projects, or for all of them together. Or even for himself. Whatever, or for whomever, or however—he was going to win the goddamn race.

He was surprised when the Russians took off like they did, but in a way he didn't mind. He felt so pumped up, so full of raw energy, that he didn't think it would hurt to burn a little early in the race. He felt so strong that he even decided to chase the Sunnino team after they had passed the Russians.

It did his heart good to hear Muzzin sic Jerome on him; it meant that David had the champ on edge, a fact that he might be able to use to his advantage later. He was going to win, that's all there was to it, and he had to admit that the psychological edge he seemed to have gave him a great deal of pleasure.

He looked over his shoulder to see that the rest of the breakaway group was close behind him. They weren't going to let him go today. That was fine. He didn't feel like blasting way out there by himself this time. Stay close, stay strong, and stay alert, he told himself.

He slowed down a little bit, allowing Muzzin to pass him as they crested a hill. The Cannibal gave him a diabolical grin. "It's no fun up front, is it?"

David tried to look as though he were afraid, hoping it would take off a little of Muzzin's edge. Muzzin let out a little yell and flew down the hill. David didn't let him get too far ahead. He wondered if he could conserve enough strength to beat him to the finish line today. He thought he could sprint faster—or just as fast. Yesterday he had simply worn himself out. Ride, he told himself. Just ride. He knew the altitude was going to be rough, but he also knew that it was going to be rough on everybody else, too.

For the next several miles he fell into a rhythm, drafting off his opponents, making sprints past entire teams, surging into the lead, then dropping back anonymously and letting the others go ahead. He never let himself fall further behind the leader than twenty or twenty-five meters. He took his water at regular intervals and ate a couple of bananas. If he could keep this consistency, he knew he could win.

The race was half over and there were still no surprises. Well, there wouldn't be until later, Marcus thought, gazing out the window at a majestic spire of red rock. So far the lead had changed hands several times between David, Muzzin, the Russians, Italians, and Japanese. Every nationality had a shot at it for a while, then each fell back and let another have a go. Marcus leaned back in the seat and closed his eyes, imagining himself into the race. In a little while the real hurt would start. More and more riders would drop off. "Only the strong survive," he muttered, opening his eyes again. Up ahead, at a bend in the road, there was a fat black kid standing on the shoulder, watching the racers go by. "Sarah," Marcus said.

"Huh?"

"I must be hallucinating."

"What's wrong?" She shot him a very concerned look.

He pointed to their left front. "That looks like Randolph Conrad."

Sarah looked, then nodded in amazement. "That *is* Randolph."

"Who's Randolph?" Becky asked.

Sarah slowed the van.

"What the hell is he . . ." Marcus trailed off as Dennis and his mother came into view around the corner. "I'll be . . ." He pounded his fist against the dashboard. "Mom?" he said to no one in particular. The van stopped and he gave Sarah a look. "Did you do this?" He didn't quite know how he felt about it.

"I called Dennis," she said.

He nodded, then got out of the van, and walked around to the driver's side. He stood there for a moment, looking across the road as other bicycles and vehicles raced between him and his mother.

Then she saw him. She seemed to freeze on the side of the road, staring penitently at her first-born son, a look of sad yearning on her face. Whatever bitterness he felt toward her evaporated and was blown away by the Rocky Mountain wind. His self-pity vanished, and he felt terribly sorry for her, realizing that there could be few things worse in life than losing your own child.

Then she seemed to grow frantic with her desire to get across the road to him, stepping out on the pavement as the vehicles continued to roar by and blast their horns at her. Dennis took her arm, looking for a hole he could run interference through. But the traffic kept coming, and finally she broke away and bolted across the road, nearly getting nailed by another van.

Her face contorted with grief and love, she ran toward Marcus, her arms outstretched. "Marcus!" she cried.

"Mom!" He felt a combination of joy at seeing her and fear that she would be splattered all over the pavement.

She stopped a foot in front of him, pulling her arms back against herself as though she needed permission from Marcus before she could touch him.

He reached out. She collapsed in his arms. "Oh, Marcus!" she cried. "I'm so sorry."

"It's okay, Mom. It's okay." He hugged her tightly, then, suddenly feeling weak, backed against the van for support.

"Why didn't you tell me?" she pleaded.

"I guess I tried," he said. "But things kept getting in the way." He waved as Dennis and Randolph ran across the road.

"Hey!" Dennis said, trying to be jovial.

"Hi, Denny." Marcus smiled warmly. "How you doin', Randolph?"

"Hi, Marcus."

Dennis gave him an apologetic look. "Hey, man, I hope you don't mind all this."

"I'm touched. Really."

"Good enough, then," Dennis said.

Marcus gestured toward the road. "But David's racing, so let's get in the van and chase him."

Dennis gave Sarah a little wave, then pointed back to his rented car. "Randolph and I'll take the car."

"See you after the race." He took his mother's arm and led her around to the other side of the van. "You're coming with *us*, Mom."

She looked a little scared. "Where are we going?"

"Up to the finish line. Your son just might win this race." He opened the door and let her into the van.

"You're Sarah," Mrs. Sommers said before David could introduce them.

"I'm real happy to meet you, Mrs. Sommers." Sarah gestured to Becky. "This is Becky."

Marcus climbed up on the seat. "Ladies, I would like you to meet my mother."

"I'm glad to meet you both." Marcus had never seen her smile quite so warmly.

David wiped the sweat from his forehead and looked to the side as both McCrary and Yamashita disappeared behind him, done for as far as this race was concerned. Stage Three was three-quarters finished, and David was hot and tired and in pain. So what? he asked himself, remembering when Marcus had said the same thing to him when they were training. Pain and fatigue were meaningless at this point. Everybody had them; the winners were the ones who held on, pushing through, transcending.

The Russians had continued to push the pace all through the race, and so far only one of the five Soviets had faded. Belov was still going like a bull, he and Muzzin swapping the lead continually. But whenever they looked back, David was there, indefatigable.

David was sure that his presence irritated Muzzin, but at this stage of the race it was the Russian that drew the lion's share of The Cannibal's ire. As they labored up a hill, Belov a couple of feet in front, Muzzin said, "I'm still here, Belov, right on your red ass."

Belov said nothing. David thought it was foolish to talk at this altitude and at this stage of exhaustion, but maybe the needling would cause Belov to make a strategic error. David hoped the countries' leaders wouldn't talk this way in a nuclear confrontation.

"I'm still behind you, Belov," Muzzin said again. "But I'm really two seconds ahead."

"Are you nuts?" Jerome wheezed.

"What do you mean?"

"He can't understand English."

"He understands. Don't you, Belov?"

The Russian continued to labor up the hill, seemingly unaware of Muzzin's taunts.

"You know why you won the Olympics, don't you? Because I wasn't there."

David was actually beginning to enjoy the monologue. It broke up the monotony.

"Well, I'm here now, Belov." Muzzin inched forward until his front wheel passed Belov's rear. "Only I'm not here," Muzzin continued. "I'm two seconds ahead."

Finally Belov shook his head angrily and took off, Golyadkin and Titov sprinting by Muzzin and blocking his way.

David winced as Muzzin pushed one of the Russians aside—the Soviet *was* crowding him a little too closely—then David shot through the gap with Jerome. Jerome looked at David and shook his head, seemingly near the end of his tether. It doesn't matter, David thought. It doesn't matter. He pumped on.

Dennis Conrad eased his rented car down the mountain road, passing some of the racers who had fallen off the pace. He felt horrible that Marcus wasn't out here, but at least there was the consolation that Marcus's little brother was doing well. Dennis looked over at Randolph who was gazing out the window with a blank expression on his face.

"Randolph?"

"Huh?"

"You notice anything unusual?"

"Yeah."

"What?"

Randolph yawned. "I have jet lag."

"That's great." He reached over and tapped him on the thigh. "There's no black riders out there."

Randolph nodded.

"Think about it."

"Maybe they're all in cars with the smart people."

Dennis glared at his son.

Randolph shrugged. "Hey, Dad, lighten up. I don't even have a bicycle."

Dennis smiled. "Your birthday's coming up."

Randolph shook his head as they passed three more gasping riders. "I still want a bowling ball, Dad. Now more than ever."

David inched ahead of Jerome, actually gaining on Muzzin and Belov who were still sprinting full-out. They finally slowed the pace, and when they were both sitting comfortably in their saddles, David took off. He stood up and sprinted past them, taking a fraction of a second to catch both of their amazed looks. Unknown Sommers, unknown equation.

"Shit!" was Muzzin's summary of David's move.

Belov grunted something in Russian. David could pretty well guess the meaning. If he hadn't been breathing so hard, he would have smiled.

"Go get him, Belov," Muzzin said.

"You get him," Belov said with a thick accent. Muzzin was right; the Russian did understand English.

"Jerome!" Muzzin commanded.

David looked back over his shoulder. Jerome was shaking his head at Muzzin. The poor guy had had it.

"Son of a bitch!" Muzzin yelled.

This time David didn't need to glance back to know that The Cannibal was making his move to eat him up.

"Those poor boys," Mrs. Sommers said, looking out the window at a quartet of exhausted bikers.

"That's what happens, Mom." Marcus looked down, managing a little smile when he saw that Sarah was holding his mother's hand. He fiddled with the radio a little more, bringing in the announcer once again.

"Ladies and gentlemen, there are ten miles to go and David Sommers is trying to steal the race from Muzzin and Belov. They are chasing hard, and this last few miles will see many riders dropping by the wayside as the lack of oxygen grows more and more severe."

Mrs. Sommers patted her chest. "I feel it myself," she said.

"Think about your son."

"Is he really in the lead?"

Marcus shrugged. "That's what the man said." The radio signal faded again, and Marcus pounded the dash futilely. "Come on," he said. "Let's catch up."

Sarah nodded, accelerating slightly.

"It's beautiful up here," Mrs. Sommers said. "I'm glad you decided to take David with you."

''Me too,'' Marcus said.

''There they are!'' Becky pointed out the front window. ''He's still up there.''

Marcus shook his head, amazed and gratified that David was still at the head of the pack. His heart went out to all of them, even The Cannibal. He knew that what they were riding on now was sheer heart and will power.

Marcus touched his nose and his finger came away bloody. He quickly wiped it on a handkerchief which he stuffed in his pocket.

His mother saw. ''Oh, Marcus!''

He pointed toward David. ''He's going all out early, Mom. He's really giving his best.''

''Should I stay back here?'' Sarah asked.

''No.'' Marcus shook his aching head. ''Let's get on to the finish line. If he had any mechanical trouble now he'd never catch up anyway.'' God, he felt horrible. He wanted to crawl in the back and lie down, but he was going to see the end of this race if it killed him. It was his only way of staying in it.

''Marcus,'' his mother said.

He patted her arm. ''It's okay, Mom.''

Sarah beeped the horn as the van went by the lead pack. Marcus and Becky leaned out the window and waved, shouting encouragement. David seemed to look right at them, then right through them. He was leading by a few feet, and the concentration on his face was incredible. Tears of pride filled Marcus's eyes. He felt a hand on his back.

''I love you, Marcus.''

He turned and gazed at his mother, unable to believe what he had just heard. She had really said it! The cool, professional Mrs. Sommers had just told her son she loved him, in front of God, the mountains, and two relatively strange women. He kissed her on the cheek.

''I tried to tell you before. I even called Wisconsin after you'd left on your trip. I . . .''

He put his fingers to her lips. She seemed too desperate. ''It's okay, Mom. Everything's okay now.''

''Will you ever forgive me?''

"I have." He kissed her on the forehead. "I love you, too."

All David could do was blink as the van went past him. He thought he saw his mother inside. She could be real, but then again, she could be an hallucination. He didn't know and he didn't have the energy to care or to think about it one way or the other. The thin air tore through his lungs, and his legs felt as if they weighed a hundred pounds apiece. Muzzin crept past him, then Belov and Golyadkin. Let them go, David thought, looking ahead at the van as it blinked out of sight around a turn. Marcus was in there, heading for the finish line to watch him come in. He picked up the pace, thinking of the film of last year's race when Marcus had given up in the final seconds. Marcus was right; it was time for a new family tradition.

He caught Muzzin and the Russians. They all slowed for a moment, then David took off into the lead. He glanced back to see Belov following. Golyadkin was shot. Then Muzzin came on, too.

Muzzin and Belov caught him, and for a moment the three of them rode abreast, each seemingly waiting for the other to make a move. David imagined that they were probably the three most tired men in the world.

David seized the initiative, standing up and sprinting for a few yards, taking the lead. He eased off, then Belov was beside him, wheezing like some used-up engine that was about to explode. David let him go, but when Muzzin went by, David jumped on his wheel.

Muzzin pulled up even with Belov, and both of them slowed down. David's desire was to do the same, but by now he knew better. He took off once again.

Belov's groan was unmistakably a groan of despair—the Russian had used himself up. David didn't even have to look back to know it. He also didn't need to look back to know that Muzzin was chasing him furiously.

A few seconds later The Cannibal pulled up beside him. David glanced over his shoulder. Belov had dropped. "We got him, kid," Muzzin rasped.

David glanced at him, saying nothing, continuing to pedal.

"Take it easy now," Muzzin said. "We work together. You got second place locked up."

David nodded deferentially. "Okay." He let Muzzin take the lead, then quickly pulled out his water bottle, took a drink and poured some of the cool liquid over his head. He put the bottle back in the cage and rode on, sucking The Cannibal's wheel.

For a moment, his mind drifted as he was struck with the raw beauty of where they were. The sky was a dark blue, and wisps of clouds hung over the gorge to his left, so close he could nearly reach out and touch them. He was at the top of the world, and despite the heavy breathing of both himself and Muzzin, and despite the noise of their bikes, he sensed a silence up here that was profound and otherworldly. A good place for an aspiring Shinto to spend some time alone in contemplation. But probably not the greatest place to be isolated with a cannibal.

David tensed as Muzzin's hand reached for his water bottle. The second the bottle touched his lips, David took off, sprinting past him with no intention of looking back.

"Son of a bitch!" Muzzin gasped.

David knew that Muzzin had tossed the bottle by now and was bearing down on him. Let Muzzin beat him—if he could.

David's peripheral vision picked up Muzzin's front wheel, then he felt something on his shoulder. He jerked, looking over to see Muzzin's angry face right next to his. "Okay, Sommers," he croaked. "I gave you your chance." He clamped his chin over David's shoulder and began forcing him to the left of the road.

For a moment, David was filled with utter terror. His bike was inches from the shoulder of the road, and the shoulder was only a few feet from a lethal gorge. He leaned to his right, trying to keep balanced, but Muzzin was much bigger than he was. The Cannibal grunted ferociously, moving David over, centimeter by centimeter.

David's bike slid onto the shoulder. Muzzin relaxed the

pressure just enough so that David could get back on the road. Muzzin grunted again, even more fearfully this time. Then David's terror slid away. He suddenly knew that Muzzin wasn't trying to kill him, that The Cannibal was simply trying to scare him to death, to make him too afraid to win the race. David could sense Muzzin's fatigue, and the thought of it gave him the last bit of energy he needed.

He gazed off at one of the mountain peaks rising in the distance, took a deep breath, and suddenly lashed out with his right arm, just as he had seen Muzzin do to the Russians who were blocking his path.

Muzzin groaned with more disbelief than pain, and wobbled off to the side. David stood up and sprinted. He looked back after about fifteen seconds. Muzzin was standing up and sprinting, too. But David was widening the gap! He had him! He had The Cannibal on the ropes! He faced front and flew toward the finish.

Sarah drove over the finish line, through an anxious sea of spectators, and pulled off at a small parking area reserved for race officials and VIPs. The guard waved and nodded as Marcus got out of the van. He turned as his mother started to follow him out, watching Sarah as she took her arm. "I think Marcus wants to be alone," she whispered. Marcus nodded gratefully, turned and started down toward the finish line.

I probably should have had a wheel chair, he thought, trying to keep his dignity as he walked slowly along. He was wearing David's cowboy hat, and he tipped the brim, like a baseball player who had just hit a home run, to several well-wishers. His body amazed him; yesterday it was full of more strength and energy than most people would ever have. And today its betrayal was nearly complete. A two-year-old probably had more strength than he did.

He stopped at the finish line for a moment, reliving last year's finish for a few seconds. He shook his head. At least he'd beaten Muzzin on Stage One; he hadn't folded at the crucial moment.

But now the moment belonged to David. Marcus eased down the hill another thirty yards. He had an odd thought—

almost a superstition—that he could give David the necessary moral support for the last few seconds of the sprint. Foolish, he thought. David was going to win this baby on his own.

Marcus stumbled and nearly fell, but regained his balance and planted his shoes on the side of the road. He took a deep breath and winced as another stab of pain tore through his head. He shook it off, giving himself over to the electric feeling in the crowd. "Come on, David," he mumbled, taking off the hat. "Come on, little brother."

"Here they come! Here they come!" The shout was passed up the hill, then he saw the flash of David's blue jersey. The PA crackled with static.

"Ladies and gentlemen, David Sommers is in the lead as they come around the corner, but even if he crosses the line first, Barry Muzzin still has an eleven-second time advantage on him overall. If Muzzin crosses the line less than eleven seconds after Sommers, Muzzin will still be the winner of the Hell of the West."

Marcus couldn't take his eyes off the race to look at his watch, but he counted off at least ten seconds in his mind before Muzzin came around the corner in his yellow jersey. "Come on, David!" he bellowed. He waved the hat frantically, knowing that this was the toughest way for David to win. Being out in front could give him a false sense of security. "Go, David. Go!" He nearly shouted the words in David's face as his brother sprinted by. Little, hell. The guy was a giant.

Their eyes locked for a moment, then Marcus turned away to look at Muzzin. The Cannibal was coming on, but not as strong as Marcus had imagined. He was whipped. Whatever the outcome of the total race, David had beaten Muzzin soundly today.

"Sommers is finished, ladies and gentlemen. Muzzin has eleven seconds to cross the line or take second."

Marcus whirled as the roar went up from the crowd. The extra seconds began ticking off on a digital clock beside the finish line, each one sending an electric jolt through Marcus's heart.

"Four," the announcer said, "three, two, one, zero. He didn't make it."

Too weak to jump for joy, Marcus clenched his fist and began walking toward the finish line.

"Ladies and gentlemen, David Sommers is the winner today! And he has captured the Hell of the West. David Sommers, First Place, Barry Muzzin, Second."

Marcus toiled up the hill toward the finish line, not knowing if he would make it or not. The effort to walk was immense, but he kept going, a wide smile on his face.

The crowd surged forward, obscuring David, keeping only a small path open for the straggling racers. Marcus walked a few more steps, then stopped and coughed into his handkerchief. Ten more steps, each one a separate agony. He looked up, but was still unable to see David. He lowered his head and continued on.

As he crossed the finish line he looked up again, and this time they were all standing there, Sarah, Becky, his mother and the latest winner of the Hell of the West. Exhausted as he was, David grabbed his mother's arm and started toward Marcus.

After they had taken a couple of steps, he gestured for them to stop. He wanted to get to them on his own. He took three more steps, then gestured for David to raise his arms.

David did, tentatively at first, but finally he put them all the way into the air.

Marcus clapped twice, took a couple of steps forward, then faltered.

David clenched his fists. "Sommers!" he said.

A wave of emotion gusted over Marcus, and he lowered his head as his eyes misted with tears. Then he looked up and clenched his own fist. "Sommers!" he echoed, and with a tremendous effort, he made the last step to his mother and his brother.

"That's it," a photographer said, brandishing his camera. "Get the whole family together."

But his words drifted away, Marcus hearing only the sound of the family name. He slid one arm around David, the other around his mother.

"That's great," the photographer said, stalking them as though they were prize game.

Marcus looked from his mother to his brother. It was as though he had been living all his life for this moment. He felt like he was holding them up, even as they supported him.

"That'll look great in the morning papers," the photographer said.

"I believe it will," Marcus croaked.

Both David and his mother hugged him closely.

"I truly believe it will," he said.